Write On...

A collection of stories, memoirs, and poems

By 23 Wichita area authors

All proceeds of this book go to
Senior Services Inc. of Wichita, KS
A not-for-profit charity.

Starla
ENTERPRISES, INC.

For information regarding permission, write to Starla Enterprises, Inc.

Attention: Permissions Department,

9415 E. Harry St., Ste. 603, Wichita, KS 67207

First Edition

ISBN: 978-1-979-03657-3

Compiled by Starla Criser

Editor & Cover Design by Starla Criser

Cover Photography by Gerald McCoy

Printed in the U.S.A.

All proceeds of this book go to Senior Services Inc. of Wichita, KS, a not-for-profit charity

LIST OF CONTRIBUTORS
and Entry Locations

TABLE OF CONTENTS

AH, TO BE A WRITER
Starla Criser

Haunted by characters demanding to have life
Dialogue swirling in your head
Settings flashing before your eyes
Conflict churning in your gut

Dreams, night and day…dreams

Emotions…show them
Backgrounds…reveal them
Senses…feel them
Plots…reveal them

Day and nights…dreams

Stories of love and romance
Chronicles of history and intrigue
Tales of fantasy and adventure
Yarns of cunning villains and wily detectives

Dreams, always dreams

Battling the blank screen, the empty page
First drafts
Sagging middles
Revisions, submissions, revisions

Dreams…slowly becoming reality

THE TEACHERS
E. L. Morrow

It was a hot August afternoon. I was working in the makeshift office, at home, when our dog came to the door and "whined." This caught my attention because this dog, a corgi named Phoenix, almost never whines.

Having my attention, he gave me a "come with me look." His concern became evident when we reached the bathroom door.

Ginger, our cat, took advantage of the cool ceramic tiled floor of the bathroom by lying across the door opening. The placement assured her that no one would close the door without her knowing it. Felines want doors to be open.

The issue involved the common water bowl located on that same tiled floor a few feet away. The four-legged ones had established unambiguous rules years before. One rule was about food. If it was eatable and in reach, it belonged to the dog. To think otherwise was to risk at least a menacing growl, if not a snap.

In return for all the food in the world, the dog agreed not to jump over the cat. It seemed like a fair trade until the dog was thirsty and the cat was blocking access to the only water in the world. A standoff ensued.

Ginger ignored Phoenix's pleas.

So, the dog invoked another rule: When you can't get what you want, ask one of the two-legged creatures for help.

What happened next was a lesson in diplomacy.

I asked Ginger to let the dog get to the water dish. She said, "ok" and stood up. But there was no place for her to go without getting trapped in the room behind the water dish. Each animal had allotted the other a space of at least two feet. The dog somehow realized the problem and knew the cat had to come where he stood.

Phoenix retreated four feet, allowing Ginger a place to go, still leaving two feet between them. The dog passed to the water dish.

It got better.

The corgi drank water for a long time. Then the cat got tired of waiting and returned to her place at the door—this time facing the dog as he drank.

Saved from death by thirst, Phoenix turned and took one step toward the door, saw the cat and jumped back. Without a word from me, bark or any other indication except that the dog wanted to leave—Ginger got up and returned to her previous holding spot. The dog left without delay, and the feline went in and drank from the same dish.

As I reflected on this incident, it became clear that our "dumb animal" friends had found a way to respect each other. It was simple: give space for the other.

How hard would it be for us "big brained" creatures to do the same? Suppose we granted not only physical but also emotional and spiritual "space" to others?

What if we all decided: even if I disagree with you, and what you think—I still allow you your opinion? We could go further. What if I decided to listen to your opinion—so I can better understand your experience and reasoning?

I would need to draw one line anytime another violated my "emotional space" by trying to force me to adopt his or her idea unthinkingly.

Such an attitude would allow us to learn from people who are very different from us. What if we considered their ideas as a "cat" that should be given space, or as a "dog" needing to get to the water?

If we do that, we might find ourselves building up the common good of all.

There are times when all three species in our home occupy a closer space. Cat curled up next to the dog, at our feet, or next to us on the couch, while reading or watching TV. The cat cleans the dog's ears, and the dog defends his sister against strays when on our walks.

Lessons are where we find them. From others, and our pets. Anyone can be our teacher.

THOUGHT OF TODAY
C. Holden

Stop and say "Hi" on your way by

No matter how you feel, life is real

Sometimes by chance, life goes by at a glance

In just a moment or two, I was thinking of you

It might have been in a passing thought or a short dream,

Or maybe on a rainbow, or a sunbeam

Life is real, and as time goes by,

Just stop for a moment and just say "Hi"

ROAD TRIP
Gwendolyn Eldridge Gandy

If you feel frustrated because most of the mail that you receive now is from AARP The Magazine and retirement communities and is piling up on your coffee table, you are not alone.

I, Shirley Smith, will turn ninety years old in August, just a few months away. I still feel radiant… hot…flashy…and glowing. Or is that hot flashes and sweating at my age? Whatever.

I still have my hair (gray) and teeth, but the right hip and both knees aren't totally original. My dance moves are a little wobbly now, but who cares if a jerk here and there can get me across the dance floor. As they say, "Age is only a number. You feel as good as you act."

***

My best friend Carol Parker, whom I have known since first grade, has always been my buddy. We have spent our lives in the same town, our children grew up together, and we lost our husbands within three years of each other. She and I not only have a lot of history together, but also share the same birthday, August thirty-first.

Carol is a delightful person. She is sunny, happy and toothless, when she forgets to put in her dentures. I also like that she is easygoing and mellow.

***

"On the road again. On the road again. I can't wait to get on the road again." I have been singing that song all morning.

Last night Carol and I talked about how we would like to celebrate our ninetieth birthdays together. I came up with the idea of a road trip. Carol said yes, why not. Excited about the idea, she started walking around the room, with her thinking cap on, face beaming and eyes rolling around. This is how she does her best thinking.

She thought for a while. Then with her best toothless smile, she looked at me and said, "Las Vegas." She reminded me this was on our Fun Places to Visit Bucket List.

The wave of excitement hit me.

Face it, at our age there's not a lot of time left to complete our list…and still remember the two big Ws: What and Where. Most of time we have a hard time remembering what happened earlier in the day. Heck! We may not even remember this plan unless we write it down. We have a Remembering Plan Book for every day, so we won't forget what plans we have made.

I said, "I will get the luggage out of the attic, so we can start our packing."

I drug the luggage down to the kitchen. It had a stale smell because I had not used it for twenty years. I would have to clean it up before putting our clothes inside. Carol offered to spray the luggage with her new perfume, but I told her no. I had something else to use that would take care of the smell.

***

Carol and I decided to brush up on our dance moves. There are the "Mashed Potato Time," the "Harlem Shuffle," and that new one they do at the senior center the "Electric Slide." I said, "If we want to be with the In crowd, we need to practice."

Carol said, "I want to be one of the hot chicks on the dance floor. I don't want to look like I am from a hick town and don't know how to dance."

***

Today is our packing day. There are only two more days before we leave on our trip. I don't know if all our things will fit into one large bag. I will really to try to make it work. Trying to take care of Carol and several pieces of luggage might be more than even I can handle. I know all the clothes will fit. Our jumpsuits, Palazzo pants, tops to match, nightgowns, and shoes. The hard part will be fitting in all the extras. These include heating pad, neck pillow, two packages of Depends, cushioned toilet seat, knee pillows, a walker, and a cane. Oh, let's not forget our pills, dentures, hearing aids, and glasses. When you are old and someone says only take the necessities, they have no idea of how much that is, but we do. Wow! We will have to take more than one large bag.

After all the packing, I am tired and ready for a nap. Carol is also tired. She watched a couple of TV shows and kept up her dancing. I didn't want her help with the packing. It would have been a big mess and a headache for me.

⋆

The big day is here! The car is packed and ready. The house is checked and locked. Carol is buckled in.

I put the car in gear and we are off. We are driving on Highway 54 so we can count the number of Mac D's between Wichita, Kansas and Las Vegas, Nevada. This will be the best ninetieth birthday ever.

"What happens in Vegas, stays in Vegas," I remind Carol.

⋆

P.S.

As we're driving along, I silently hope that we don't have to show our driver's license at any of the clubs…or anywhere along the way. Because we don't have one.

"On the road again. I can't wait to get on the road again."

UNFINISHED
Connie Holt

In the movies, when someone dies—
You get a chance to say "goodbye,"
They linger enough for you to say
How much you've loved their little ways
Of touching others' lives and then,
They leave you with a last sigh and grin.

You left this earth one day at dusk.
How could I know? How could I trust?
That when I saw you turn to leave,
When next we met, 'twould be in grief.
Your lifeless body sweetly lay,
Too late to hug, too late to say
How much your smile caressed my day.

Now you laugh and sing, and run and play,
Forever young, the angels say.
When next I see your smiling face,
I will be Home, by God's Free Grace.

BITTERSWEET
Bunnie Clark

The gray skies threatened rain the day Dad and I went to the carnival. I didn't care; I was so excited to have a new experience. I had never been to a carnival before. Skipping along on the gravel road, I kicked at rocks with my new red shoes.

Dad said, "Be careful, sweetie, you don't want to scuff up those shoes and get me in trouble with Mom." But he laughed when he said it. His brown eyes filled with love for me.

I looked up at my dad, so tall and strong, so handsome. On this warm day, his coat was tossed over his shoulder like some famous movie star would do. That's how handsome my dad was.

As we got closer to the fairgrounds, I heard music coming from all directions. And the noise, oh my! People laughing and shouting, Kids running and screaming as their parents yelled at them to wait, slow down. I crept closer to Dad. The noise, the crowd and colors all blending together was unsettling. I reached for his hand as we continued down the boardwalk. I felt safe with Dad, but still.

I saw booths loaded with toys, stuffed animals, balls and balloons. Suddenly, I stopped. When Dad looked down at me, I pointed to a booth with stuffed animals. I began to tug on his hand and pull him in that direction. At that booth, a huge teddy bear looked straight at me. He wanted me to take him home and get him away from all that noise and confusion.

When we reached the stand, I stood on my tiptoes to see the big man who manned the booth. I only saw his eyes and nose because he was the hairiest man I had ever seen…and the scariest. Even that wasn't enough to back me away from my Teddy.

Dad could see how much I craved that toy. He shrugged and said, "Well, let's give it a try."

Mr. Hairy Man gave Dad three wooden balls and said, "You gotta knock down all six a dem pins. An dat'll be $2.00."

Dad handed me his coat and dug into his pocket for some bills. I jumped up and down with excitement. I had no doubt that my dad could knock 'em all down.

He threw the first ball and only one plunked over with a loud thunk. With the second ball, he got two of 'em. I held my breath as he threw the third ball. Two went over this time. One left standing.

I hung my head and tears threatened to well in my eyes. But no, Dad dug into his pocket again and pulled out two more bills.

He looked at me and winked. "I just needed to warm up," he told me.

Mr. Hairy handed Dad three more balls. I could tell he didn't think Dad had a chance. But he didn't know my dad.

Dad wound his arms around a couple of times, and let the ball go with all his might. That ball hit "dem" pins and they went flying all over the place. They made so much noise it startled the people around us. They looked in our direction just as Mr. Hairy picked up my teddy and handed it to me. The crowd cheered and clapped.

We turned, headed for home. I had all the excitement I could stand for one day.

The sky threatening rain earlier had become cloudy and the wind blew stronger. Dad grabbed my hand and we ran. The last thing we needed was for the roads to turn to mud. We didn't want to take a chance on my new red shoes getting muddy. And my teddy, his beautiful brownish orange fur mustn't get wet.

The clouds burst at the same time we rushed through our front door. We were laughing and out of breath from our race with the weather.

Mom met us at the door ready to towel us off if we had gotten wet. She laughed when she saw my teddy bear. "Welcome to the family," she said to my Teddy. I had not yet named my bear, because I wanted to introduce him to my kitten first.

Daffodil was a tiny stray that we found a few years ago. Or maybe she found us. Anyway, she showed up on our porch all skinny and bedraggled. Her sad yellow eyes just begged to be taken in. And of course, we had. Mom had told me I needed to name her. It had been spring and flowers were beginning to pop their heads out of the ground. So, "Daffodil" fit her perfectly. Mostly yellow with yellow eyes, she had a brown stripe around her neck that made her look as though she wore a necklace. She was my best friend. I wanted to let her know that she wasn't being replaced. However, she would have to share our room with Mr. Teddy.

The rain was short lived. The next morning, I took Mr. Teddy and Daffodil outdoors for dress up time. I wore Mom's floppy straw hat that had a purple flower on it. We liked to sit under a favorite willow tree. Its long, flexible limbs and mossy like leaves drooped to the ground. We could be hidden from the world and shielded from the wind and hot sun. I was happy to show Mr. Teddy our special secret place. Daffodil didn't seem to mind, especially since she had just discovered a lizard as green as a pickle.

I watched her carefully, ready to rescue the lizard if I saw that it was in danger. Lucky for Mrs. Lizard, she sensed the danger and skittered away.

***

I lost my first tooth. It was exciting because I had heard about the tooth fairy bringing gifts and coins. I didn't know if it was true, but I wanted to find out. After Mom pulled my tooth—ugh—which hung by a thread, she put it in a glass beside my bed. She didn't know what the tooth fairy did either. Mom had heard they only came at night when you were sleeping.

It was broad daylight outside with the sun shining. How was I going to wait until bedtime?

Oh well, I figured I might as well go play. It had rained a couple of days before, washing the skies into a beautiful blue color. The rain had brought the frogs out and I heard them splashing away in the pond. Mom made me a honey and peanut butter sandwich and grapes for a picnic lunch.

While I munched on my snack sitting under my favorite willow tree, I dreamed about what the tooth fairy might bring me. And what exactly did the tooth fairy look like? Pretty and dainty like a doll, or a big hairy troll who would take my tooth and leave nothing? Mom said my imagination was bigger than me and it would get me in trouble.

I wondered if my imagination really was getting me into trouble. Because it seemed to me like the blue in the sky turned a strange green. The wind was beginning to blow and the willow branches swayed and dipped way low to the ground. I felt a few drops of rain coming through the tree. Maybe the bad tooth fairy troll was coming early. Maybe he took my gift from the dainty little fairy and he raged through the skies. The idea frightened me. As far as I was concerned, he could have the darned tooth.

Through the noise of the wind, I heard Mom yelling, "Twister! Twister! Come quickly to the cellar."

As I ran from under the shelter of the tree, I felt freezing rain drops hitting me hard. I ran toward the sound of my mother's voice. Was the troll called Twister? It made no sense to me, but I wasn't stopping until I got to Mom.

We scurried down the steps of the cellar. It was creepy there, but I felt safer inside with Mom. Outside the troll howled and stomped around like a wild buffalo. Mom had grabbed a yellow shawl as she ran from the house and threw it around my shaking, cold body.

I pulled her close and whispered in her ear, "Can the bad tooth fairy get in here?"

"Goodness, whatever are you talking about? There is no such thing as a bad tooth fairy."

What? There was no bad tooth fairy? I thought he was outside trying to get me.

"No, sweetie, it's a storm that came up quickly. I think it is over now. Let's go up and see."

The cellar was hot and made me sweat. Even though I feared what was outside, I wanted to leave that hole in the ground with the black scary shadowy things lurking in the corner. I scrambled up the stairs only to fall and skin my knee on the steps. Disappointed with the way the day was spinning out of control, I began to cry. The storm probably blew away my tooth and the good fairy.

Mom opened the door to the cellar. I didn't know what we would see, but with the way my life was going right now, I didn't expect to see anything good. The willow drooped from the weight of the water but it was still standing.   A few twigs had fallen from it and littered the ground. I could still hide under it. One of Dad's old toolsheds had crumpled like a folded-up tent.   A clock that Dad was going to repair peeked out from under the pile with its little hands all pointed in the wrong directions. That old shed was going to need more than a paint job.   That's what my dad said every year, "Got to give that toolshed a paint job this year."

***

Today would be a brand-new adventure. We were going on a trip. And best of all, a bus trip. I had never been on a bus before. I shivered in excitement every time I thought about it. I watched the clock as the hours ticked by. I got up early this morning, while it was silent and dark outside.

Mom and Dad didn't move in bed. How could they sleep? I had already started packing my suitcase. Had I missed anything important? My blue swimsuit for the beach, my rain jacket, just in case, and the yellow hat with the red rose. which my granny bought for me. She would be happy to see me wearing that.

We go see Granny every summer. Our old truck was broken and Dad said it might not make it all the way. He wasn't taking any chances on ruining our trip. Besides, he said, it would be great to sit back and let someone else do the drivin'.

The sun was coming up. I thought it would be a perfect day. Finally, Mom and Dad were packed and ready to go, too. Mom was bringing a lunch for us because it would be a long trip. She knew me and Dad would be hungry.

Here comes the bus! Here comes the bus! I jumped up and down like a frog.

When the bus came to a stop, I leaped on the steps and climbed into the bus as fast as I could. I grabbed the seat by the window and pressed my face against the glass.

Mom laughed and said, "There will be a lot to see. Don't be so wiggly you will be worn out before we get there."

And she was so right. There had been a lot to see. We rode close to a huge lake. I was excited to see a sailboat far away in the distance. I wondered how far it would sail. I craned my head around and watched the boat until it looked like a toy in the water.

The countryside whizzed by so quickly. Some cars came towards us fast, others going in the opposite direction. With the road stretching ahead of us, I began to imagine where the people in those cars might be going. Were they families like ours going to visit their granny? Or maybe they were heading toward that big lake to go fishing. My daddy loved to fish. When he went to our pond, he always said, "I'm comin' home with a big ole' catfish for your Mama to fry up for us."

About when my tummy began to make gurgling noises, the bus rolled to a stop. It was time for the lunch Mom had packed for us. I was as happy to get off the bus as I was to get on it. Hungry, I wanted to get outside and look around. It looked like we had stopped at a park, with a tent and some picnic tables inside. It was getting a little windy, with a chill in the air. BRRR. It was good to get inside the tent for our lunch.

After lunch, I explored the little park, looking at the flowers and listening to the birds. When it was time to get back on the bus, I was tired and drowsy. I tried to keep my eyes open, but soon I had drifted to sleep, dreaming of pansies and peacocks.

I opened my eyes when the sun shone into my bedroom at Granny's house. Dad had carried me all the way from the bus to my bed. I didn't wake up even for a minute.

***

I remember that year clearly and with fondness. It was also with the most bittersweet of memories. After I had gone to bed in the evenings, I heard the radio playing. I also heard Mom and Dad and Granny talking softly far into the night. The war was far away and far removed from me. However, it was closer than I knew.

When we returned home, Dad joined the military. Mom and I walked into town with him, where he boarded a bus that would take him away from us. We held hands all the way home—not talking much—where we waited for Dad to come back.

AN AGING BEAUTY
Starla Criser

Her tender young face eager,
hair fluffy and bouncing,
skin rosy and almost flawless,
body firm and healthy,
the child pretends and dreams
of her future beauty.

Her youthful face optimistic,
hair robust and glowing,
skin tan and nearly perfect,
body soft and fit,
the teenager hopes and dreams
of becoming a beauty.

Her mature face sorrowful,
hair uncooperative and graying,
skin aging and no longer unblemished,
body sagging and less strong,
the woman frets and dreams
of her fading beauty.

Her wrinkled face thoughtful,
hair lifeless and thinning,
skin withered and lined,
body shrinking and weaker,
the aged woman muses and dreams
of yesterday's beauty.

Yet in God's eyes,
and in those of who love her,
she has always been a beauty,
will forever be a beauty.

BEAUTY: GOD'S LOVE IN MOTION
Nancy Breth

The day of our own private showing of "Beauty: God's Love in Motion," my daughter Carrie and I were on a trek—to find clothes that fit.

She had called a few days before feeling really down hearted after a trip to Towne East Mall. She had searched for an outfit or two to wear on her anniversary trip, but found only size "A" (anorexic) clothes in the styles she liked. Carrie is shaped like a woman, with hips; round, soft-to-the-touch and healthy looking. She has a booty to shake, unlike those bony models that can only rattle their bones when showing off their womanly bodies.

"I'm so depressed," she wailed. "Everywhere you look all you see are size zeros, advertisements for diet foods, skinny models smiling for the camera. As if having lost every ounce of body fat is the path to Nirvana." And this coming from the happiest, most positive person I know.

"Well, we'll fix that," I fumed. Then we made a pact to find clothes, beautiful clothes that fit and showed off the curves of her gorgeous body—no matter how long it took.

We stayed away from the big malls where all the skinnies hang out. We had hoped to find a "Hips R Us." Alas, no such luck. We began our search at a small strip mall where we found everything she was looking for and more.

As we walked through the first store, she found blouses, skirts and pants that were stylish. And best of all, she discovered in the dressing room that they fit—glorious, hug-her-beautiful-curves fit.

Inspired by her sweet success at the first store, we bravely entered store after store, finding more clothes. Then, on to the shoes to match her new wardrobe. Our "oohs" and "aahs" and "awesomes" echoed within the walls of every clothing and shoe store on the strip, as we filled our arms with sacks full of treasure.

After all the bounty was locked safely in the car, we decided to give ourselves a treat at the café in the bookstore close by. As we sat outside in the shade slurping some kind of heavenly combination of chocolate and creamy fat calories, I was off in my usual trance. Most likely I was reviewing tomorrow's to-do list or beating myself up for something I did or didn't do the last time the two of us were together.

So Carrie saw it first. "Look, Mom. Come look at this!" There on the ledge of the bookstore window was a dragonfly so large I thought it was a hummingbird. "Ooh, aah, awesome," we were both saying.

She was so regal, a queen of the dragonflies. A sleeping beauty covered in a kaleidoscope of colors. With each blink of the eye, we saw different colors and patterns glistening from the body of this gorgeous creature. She seemed to be posing just for us—a private showing.

"Here I am in all my glory and I want to share it with you," she seemed to say. We gazed in wonder while she rested in the cool breeze of the shade.

We stood mesmerized in this silent, sacred moment until she took flight. "OK, gals, you've had enough. It's time to share myself with someone new," Her Majesty flaunted as she buzzed off.

She hovered for an instant, dazzling us with the beauty of her body in motion. Her translucent wings magnified the rays of sunlight bathing her body. Again, we held our breath while watching as she grew smaller and smaller, disappearing into the horizon.

Before returning to our table, we shared a speechless "Wow" moment as we smiled our thoughts at each other.

Now that our trek to find clothes that fit was complete, I was fully present for the rock concert as I drove Carrie home. We shared our joyful noise as we buzzed down Broadway singing "Wild Thing" at the top of our lungs with the windows rolled down.

After unloading her treasures, Carrie's family room became a fashion show runway as she modeled her new outfits for me one by one. "My honey will love this one," she said as she twirled around the room dazzling me with the beauty of that glow of love she and her husband have shared through all their years together. A glow that extends to a love for Life in all its beauty.

"Ooh, aah, awesome, what a beauty she is," I was thinking. But what I was seeing was so much more than this lovely woman showing off a few stylish outfits.

Every time I blinked my eyes, I saw a different part that makes up the whole, round, soft-to-the-touch, warm and glowing beauty that is Carrie. I saw a kaleidoscope of treasured moments with this child of mine. The tiny baby with chubby cheeks who could melt my heart with one look into those big, brown eyes. The child who had always been at peace with the world and always had a multitude of friends. The frightened child waving good-bye on her first day at school. The rebellious teenager who couldn't wait to move away from home, who also wrote books of poetry for me. The courageous woman who went on to pass her travel agent final test with 100% in the same week she caught her first fiancé in bed with another woman. I saw this wise, mature woman trembling with joy as she walked down the aisle to be married to her best friend. And I can still hear the musical joy in her voice when she shared the magic of the moment when he proposed.

I saw the broken hearts, the scrapes and scars, the laughter, the singing, the dancing, the disappointments and the successes. How through it all—the yelling and scolding and my betrayals of her trust in me, she always looked up to me, respected me, and loved me unconditionally. I saw the regal beauty in her calm, enduring strength through all the crises she has been through. The radiance of that first smile after her brain surgery, even though it hurt like hell to even blink. The lilting laughter, which soon became pounding headache when I helped her with that first shower after the bandages were off.

I saw a loving soul forged from glory and joy, and from pain and suffering; a soul that refuses to give in or to stay in the shadows. Like the dragonfly, she only knows how to fly and loves the sharing of the beauty of her flight through life. This beauty comes from God's love, a source deep within, flowing out and into the world to be given away, an eternal beauty that whether size "0" or size "40" will glow always brighter and more majestic through the years. She is Beauty. She is God's Love in Motion.

We both found beauty that day—in a smile of satisfaction reflected in the dressing room mirror, in the whirring whisper of a dragonfly's wings reminding us to be here right now, in the pulsing beat of a rock and roll song joining two voices into one, in the sacred silent peace of being aware of God's presence in every moment of our lives. All this in one day—the day of our own special viewing of "Beauty: God's Love in Motion."

A CHILD

C. Holden

A Child is

Innocence,

Love,

Adventure,

Curious,

Mischievous,

Mysterious,

Hope,

Special,

A Child Will,

Test You,

Defy You,

Argue With You,

Mock You,

Respect You,

Amuse You,

Entertain You,

Ask You,

Will Learn From You

A DOG'S LIFE IS A GOOD LIFE
Gwendolyn Eldridge Gandy

I'm Puffy, a delightfully cute little Pomeranian dog. Modest, too.

Today, I went to my monthly treat of primping and pampering time at the "Golden Bone Spa." I spent two hours being treated like the Queen I am.

Mr. Avon, the concierge at the salon, always greets me with hugs and kisses. He is a huge man, over six feet tall, with an arm span as wide as a double door. Besides his large size, he is gentle as a lamb with me, and I love him.

When I finished with my blow dry and last massage treatment, the warming drawer was opened. Out came my favorite warm, purple sweater. Mr. Avon slipped me into it so that I would be comfortable and warm on my convertible ride home.

Mr. Avon and I kissed goodbye, as always. Then I was out the door. What a dog-gone good day this had been.

LADY RED
Sharon Revell

I didn't plan to adopt another dog. The year I moved to town had been very hard. In November, my German Shepherd, Gretchen, was diagnosed with an inoperable tumor. She had been with me since she was five weeks old and was the smartest, most companionable dog I had ever known. In December, my 25-year-old Arabian mare, Charisma Jo, died. Chrissy was also perfect, wonderfully trained and beautiful. I would never know again the heavenly feeling of riding a horse whose every movement felt like an extension of your own body. But when my friend who headed a rescue group called to tell me there was an older Doberman at the shelter I should look at, I decided to go. I had owned two Dobies in past years, and knew what good dogs they were. This is Lady's story as I imagine it.

***

Lady knew it was wrong when all those strangers came into the house—her house and Ben's—and moved around as if they belonged there. She searched for Ben to tell him the strangers were opening his drawers, looking in his closet, whispering among themselves, but could not find him. Sometimes they looked at her in a fond but worried way, and shook their heads and said to each other that "I can't…my cats would just die!" or "No pets allowed in my apartment house" and "I just don't understand why he didn't find a home for her—such a nice dog. But getting old."

They did not understand the dinner rituals she and Ben had enjoyed, although they had located the bag of dog food under the sink. They eventually understood what she needed when she sat at the door to the back yard and finally (almost too late) let her out. And the most puzzling indignity—they thought that first night she would sleep in the basement! But her earnest efforts to destroy the door at the top of the stairs had soon led them to understand their mistake and she had taken her place on the rug by Ben's bed. She would guard that bed until he returned—that was her job.

Lady was kind when they bent to caress her and did not flinch from the terrible smell they carried with them—the same bad odor as the coffee can full of sand and disgusting little white stubs they put by her back

21

door. Soon Ben would return, bringing with him the fresh fragrances of the barbershop and the soap he used every morning. Until then, good manners would keep her from growling at the strangers when they burned foul little cylinders in the house—even in their mouths!—destroying all the good smells of home.

Finally, the day came when one of them took down her leash and the keys to the car and Lady realized joyfully that they were going to get Ben.

"Come on, old girl, into the back," as if she had to be told.

The car still carried Ben's scent, and she curled up happily on the back seat. But the ride to Ben's shop seemed very long that day. When finally the car stopped in front of a low cement block building, she was confused by the animal smells and sounds coming from inside.

The stranger tugged her out of the car and they walked to the door of the strange building and went inside. The deluge of smells and the cacophony of sounds were overwhelming to her delicate nose and ears. She pressed close against the man's legs while he talked to someone and filled out some papers. Then he patted her head and handed her leash to another stranger, and she understood that he was feeling sad and was not able to say goodbye.

Lady followed the new stranger through still another door and down a hall lined with cells on both sides, where dogs of every size and color, every age and breed, barked anxiously or begged with sad eyes as they passed by.

When they reached an empty cell, the stranger opened the door and led her inside, showing her that there was a blanket on the floor for her to lie upon and a bowl of water attached to the wall. Then he closed the door and went back up the hall, leaving her alone with all the sad and worried dogs.

Lady sat by the door for a while, waiting, then gave up and curled into a ball on the blanket. She tried to sleep, but the cement under the blanket was hard and cold, and the cries of the other dogs echoed in the long hall, making real rest impossible. Surely Ben would come for her soon.

The days became a week, then stretched into two weeks. Every time the door opened, she looked to see if Ben had finally come. Nearly every day, people—men, women, often children—walked up and down the hall looking at the dogs. Sometimes they commented on her beauty and elegance, but when a dog was chosen to leave with them, it would be younger or more eager to ingratiate itself. She often heard comments on the unsuitability of older dogs for young families.

On the fifteenth day, one of the kind strangers who had been feeding her every day came in with a leash (not hers—someone else's) and clipped it on her collar.

"Be a good girl now, this might just be a chance for you," he said as they walked toward the front.

In a small visiting room off the main area, a woman was sitting expectantly on a low chair, and when Lady came to the door, she said, "Well, look at you, pretty thing. Come over here." She patted her knee.

The man handed her the end of Lady's leash and said he would be back in a few minutes to see how they were getting along.

Lady sat down in front of this new stranger and they regarded each other soberly. The woman had hair of grey, not curly brown like Ben. She did not have Ben's wonderful scent, but at least she did not smell like the strangers at the house. She stroked Lady and ran her hands down Lady's front legs, all the while murmuring about cats and whether Lady was "house broke"—whatever that was.

Finally, she lifted Lady's muzzle and looked into her brown eyes. "You might just do. Would you like to come home with me?" she said, and when she stood up with the leash in her hand, Lady understood that yet another change was coming.

***

So, Lady has been here for a year now. There's some grey in her muzzle and in her eyebrows. I give her a pill every day to prevent leaking on her bedding, which she hates. She will stand outside her crate and whine for me to change her pillow, if it is slightly damp. When I laugh, she wrinkles up her nose and smiles her wolfish Dobie smile. And then I have to laugh even more and tell her how cute she is. She is always handy in case I want

23

to pet her when I sit down to watch television or read. But I say, "That's all, Lady," she trails off, either to her crate or to curl up in the bathroom.

Lady loves to ride in the car, sitting like Mrs. Astor in the back seat. Strangers have leaned out their windows at stoplights to ask if I have any more like her. Makes me proud. She has taught me that even grief has its season and will pass. And, yes, sometimes joy just bubbles up, and I feel like the luckiest old lady in the world.

SURVIVOR STORY
Rowena Hinshaw
(19-year survivor)

As a Breast Cancer Survivor, I am thankful to God, my family, friends, and doctors, before and after my diagnosis, and treatment. Many of my friends have been an encouragement to me, and I try to do the same.

My story really started at age 37, when I had my first mammogram. I did have a spot that had to be checked out (surgical biopsy), and, thankfully, it was not cancer. I continued to have regular check-ups, including yearly mammograms. I did have to have another biopsy eight years later, but it showed no cancer.

At the age of 50, in 1990, the American Red Cross was having a 5K run. I thought I could do that, since I had always been active, but not a runner, at that time. It was free to blood donors (which I was), and we would get a free T-shirt, and food after the race.

In Kansas, having a race in June, in the evening, it was hot and humid. My goal was to finish the 3.1 miles. I did that, and thought how do people run in hot weather? After that, I thought with a little training, I might be able to run in another race. Later that year, I did run in a few races, and it got easier.

In 1993, Wichita was having the Race for the Cure. I knew it was for a good cause, and I entered it, and ran the whole race. I also met survivors and was encouraged by them being there.

I continued to run every year in this race and never dreamed I would be diagnosed in May 1998 with Breast Cancer. I had successful surgery, with a mastectomy on my right side. I didn't have to have chemo, but it took several months for my right arm to function like normal. At the time of my diagnosis, I was training for the River Run (10K), and the doctor said I could run, as my surgery was in June 1998.

In that fall, I signed up for the Race for the Cure, but this time it had a new meaning for me, as I was a Survivor!

Up to 2005, I have not missed a Race for the Cure here in Wichita. Many women have said I encouraged them, as I am still running at the age of 66, and I am a survivor, too. I tell them to get annual mammograms, as early detection will save your life! My running is a good outlet for me, but everyone should take an active role in their health.

Too many women, and men, are still getting Breast Cancer each year. The research must go on until we can find a Cure.

BEFORE YOU GET OLD
C. Holden

As I sit by the window, to see the land,

In a different way than is written by hand,

It is better by sight, so I have been told

So, take a Bus ride, before you get too old!

WHEN I GET TOO OLD TO DREAM
C. Holden

Sometimes a thought is out of the blue or in a dream,

Or just a vision of places near or faraway,

We dream of things both real and fantasy,

When we get too old to dream life is over.

LOVING MOM
Nancy Breth

For months and months, I have been praying and praying to you, God, to help me to love Mom well enough through her final years. To help me let go of all this old baggage I have been carrying around all these years—you know—all this Mother/Daughter "stuff" we both keep carrying around: the guilt, the anger, the resentments and frustration—just take it all away. So it doesn't clutter up the times we spend together now.

It has been so hard watching the decline of Mom's body, and now her mind. Dementia is such a cruel fate for a lifetime of giving the all of you to your family and friends and community. To now only be able to do the simplest of tasks to take care of herself seems so unjust, God. It is so hard to find the joy beyond this deep sorrow, this anger at no longer having that mother who was always there for me and my brothers and sisters and the grandkids.

Now this great fear of what is to come has me feeling helpless, lost, and torn between wanting to be there for her no matter what, and wanting so much to experience this freedom—this awesome new joy-filled life that has been unfolding for me since I retired. What about that, God? What can I do to take good care of Mom when she is going to need round the clock care?

You keep whispering back to me after every prayer, every sleepless night trying to figure out how to be what she needs me to be when I am still so needy myself. You whisper, "Just love" and that's just too simple. How is that an answer, God? What does that really mean?

But you keep on whispering, "Just love," as if by breathing in those words I will know what to do. Now after a few thousand times (or maybe less) I am finally starting to get your message.

Today I'm here at Mom's, determined to just love her today; not be the fixer, the nurse, or the teacher. And not giving her my usual lectures about eating right, or getting up and walking more, or getting out of her room to go visit with the other ladies more (all which she has heard a jillion times from me and from my sisters). Instead, I made the choice to just love her today.

So, as I sit here holding Mom's trembling hand, waiting for the tremors to stop so I can clip her nails, I let go of all those thoughts that are usually tumbling through my mind when I am here, or when I am thinking about her and how to fix her. I am letting go and letting love take over. Instead of just getting to the task at hand, I take a moment and look deep into her eyes. And I feel a rush of pure sweet Divine Love surging through my veins. In this moment, it is as if I am seeing and knowing her; truly seeing her and knowing her for the first time.

Her nails and the shape of her fingers are long and slender like mine. So like mine it is my hand I am holding. My flesh is her flesh. We are one and the same in this tender moment. I see her holding my tiny baby hand in hers trying to gently calm the moving, and grasping long enough to clip those tiny nails so I won't scratch myself. I am also seeing myself doing the same with my babies.

In this moment, I see and know so well the loving mother she tried to be for me. I am also thinking of the loving mother I tried so hard to be for my son and daughter. How I would hold their tiny hands in mine and marvel at their flesh which came from my flesh, and how ecstatically joyful and privileged I felt to be entrusted with the care of these tiny, fragile, sacred beings who needed me so very much.

And as her hand stills and I am trying to clip the nails—in fear of bruising or cutting her fragile pale flesh, I also know the fears we as mothers have shared. Fears that we will make mistakes and hurt this child whose pain is our pain magnified, whose joy is our joy multiplied. Whose very life is so much a part of who we are we can't even imagine what we would have been without them—without this awesome and grand, frightening, all-encompassing and overwhelming Divine and Sacred Love that never stops feeling and following this tugging at the heart. These hearts that have been turned inside out; wrenched out of our chests in grief then joy, now anger then sweet forgiveness, dulling boredom then jarring excitement, cruel frustration then astonishingly peaceful acceptance.

In this one short but very sweet moment, I feel and know God's Divine and Sacred Love we are all born into and joyfully fall into when we leave this world. I see now and understand your answer, God (at least here and now in this tender moment for awhile) to just love. When I act from love, I give my whole self to just this moment. I open up my heart, instead of shutting out what I don't want to hear. I see and listen and feel—with my ears, my eyes, my hands, my entire body tuning in to this tiny, fragile sacred being who needs me being me—the daughter she knows and loves so well. She doesn't need a nurse, a teacher or fixer upper; not even some sainted being who is so pure and holy she's never thought a bad thought or complained or cursed God for the stuff that happens in her life. She needs me just loving her—letting God's Divine Love flow through each of us and into the wounded, scarred and scared places in our hearts so we can spend our final days together just loving.

WHEN YOU REALIZE THAT YOU NEED AN ESCORT TO THE DOCTOR'S OFFICE

Barbara Cairns

I had a bone density test today and had to fill out forms first. I was daydreaming and, quite frankly, deep in thoughts of my childhood. My not having completed forms in quite a while put me at a disadvantage; I was just out of practice. I Had to complete my health history and then my name. Simple, huh? Everything was going fine.

The next question was birthdate and immediately after that was height and weight. The height and weight of me when I was born? Why would they need that? I was a small baby, around five pounds, but I had no idea how long I was, and there was no one left to ask. While I was pondering these questions and how irrelevant they were, I looked at the next.

Address! I was born in Oklahoma, at home, on a farm, before they even had rural route numbers. This made me decide to carry a folder with all this information for my future doctor visits. And then, I suddenly realized that this form wanted my current information. That made better sense. What was I thinking?

As I was erasing and scratching out what I had written, I was caught. My name was called, no more time to correct my grievous errors. I had to hand in what I had written. I felt like a third grader who had not studied for a history test. The technician looked at the information I had provided and just shook his head. After the procedure, he wished me luck. I think he was concerned about my getting home safely without an escort.

I'M TRAPPED IN MY BODY AND I CAN'T GET OUT

Jan Koelsch

Inside this body is a calm person who has everything within her control. All emotions, all mental processes, spiritual aspects, and all physical capabilities come together. This inside person has a timeless look. She is a person of youth. She is slender and lithe with the figure of a Greek goddess, curves in all the right places. Muscles that perform with strength and power. Movement that creates the illusion of floating, gliding on the air. No pain. No chronic illness. No cancer. Absolute perfection. The inside person is fulfilled and satisfied and serene.

The inside person is fully aware of the capabilities and gifts that produce rewards of success in her life, in her career. The inside person knows who she is and the valued person she is. Her importance comes from internal contentment and the rewards of helping others, as well as a life well lived. The woman on the inside generates positiveness, possibilities, potential, and humor.

Spiritually the inside person loves God, trusting Him without reservation. She commits all that she is and ever hopes to be to His purpose and plan for her life. His Son, Jesus is her Savior. The Holy Spirit is her guide. She is a kind and gentle spirit, truly beautiful inside and out.

The inside person has no chronic pain, aches or hurts. Her body has never been traumatized or put in harm's way. Unscathed from anything rare or unusual. No diseases or any illnesses have ever claimed a day of her life. The inside person has no scars, no wounds, no imperfections. She is the ideal weight, height and size.

The inside person is trapped in the body of reality. She cannot get out. That is the goal, the resolution that remains to be gained, to be accomplished. The reality body is everything opposite of the inside person. Everything is not good, perfect or easy to live with. The reality body is the result of life and "boo-boos."

The reality body longs to connect with the inside person. For you see, when the communication and the connection of the two parts come together and mesh; wholeness, health and well-being in all realms will be the result. There will be peace and serenity and joy. It would be a dream come true. Life would be good.

I am both of those parts existing as one. Not an easy task. Sometimes the task becomes overwhelming as more reality is currently being added while other parts are being released or healed. The more traumas addressed, the more come forth. Almost like Lazarus coming from the grave after dying. Or like finding a needle in a haystack and the whole pile of unbaled hay tumbles down almost suffocating my very being. Pandora's box not only opened but exploded.

This reality body was never something I asked for in my life. Certainly not deserved. Quite the contrary is true. The reality body, however, is the one I have been given. Like all people, we are given only one body in our lifetime—the good, the bad, the ugly. No perfection, no wholeness. No completeness until at death we step into a new realm of a new body. Then the inside person and the reality body merge—whole, healthy and complete. I am not willing to go that path yet. I do long for the completeness and wholeness, though.

Until then, I guess I will have to learn how to cope with the reality body. I will have to uncover the layers and layers of trauma that need to be resolved. And slowly, ever so slowly and consistently one layer at a time, the reality person will become the same as the inside person.

Until then, I am trapped in my body and I cannot get out.

MARCH BIRTHDAY PARTY
Maudyne Cline

I spent a fun morning at Linwood Senior Center. I go to participate in stretching, brain games, and dynabands.

I have met many wonderful people and really enjoy the staff. I am able to read the daily newspaper, drink coffee and eat doughnuts.

Every third Wednesday of the month is our birthday celebration day.

The group leader has invited a young lady to the group to play piano and lead the singing.

The young lady, who is blind, plays rag-time, boogie, and the old favorites. She shared she was thankful for her talents, said thank you for asking her to play.

Everyone told her thank you and please return. Great day.

BM IN THE AM
C. Holden

Bran Muffins in the early morn, fresh out of a wood fired oven.

Made from a recipe your Grand Ma has and handed down by her.

Made from scratch and had mixed in a bowl
with love and care for all to enjoy!

AROUND AND AROUND

C. Holden

Around and around we go, as we rock, to and fro,

And where we stop we will not know

As around and around we go.

Life sometimes seems kind of dilly, or a little willy-nilly,

Or maybe just plain silly,

And around and around we go.

OH, THOSE GOLDEN YEARS
The Trilogy
J.M. Badger

I begin this saga by saying that I see myself as a typical grandmother these days. This morning there was an interview with Leslie Stahl of ABC's 20/20 fame. She's written a book about grandparents now that she's so excited about being one. In fact, I just called the Wichita Public Library and was told that the book is called Becoming Grandma: The Joys and Science of the New Grandparenting. It was published on April 4, 2017 and the library already has a copy.

The little aside completed, she mentioned she went about the research for this book on grandparents like she would go about the research for a story on the show.

It seems that now grandparents tend to sell their home of 40 years (mine was 46) and move closer to their grandchildren. I left home one morning to come for a visit with no idea whatsoever of buying another house. What do I do? I came home that evening having purchased a house.

This house that I saw has everything I need on one floor. There's an attached two-car garage facing a different street. You can enter the house through the laundry room, and then go into the kitchen. There's a master suite with a large bathroom and walk-in closet. The young people seem to like this house, judging by the amount of time they spend here.

The trilogy of events starts with my cordless Dyson. My daughter stopped in one day and when she noticed some granola spilled in one of the kitchen cabinets, she went to clean it up with the Dyson. Next, I hear, "Mom, you're missing a part to the Dyson. It won't work without it!"

This was news to me, so I went to investigate. Sure enough, there's a hole where I'm told the filter should be.

The Dyson is hanging in the laundry room right around the corner from the kitchen table—handy when you want to clean up crumbs! I've searched all over here for that part, even in my car where I used it. How could it disappear without my knowing about it?

A neighbor searched! Has it been found? No! A mystery.

The second part of the trilogy took place on Palm Sunday. I returned home from church to find my granddaughter had ridden her bike over here. Soon a friend of hers would ride her bike over, too.

My daughter and her best friend are in the clothing business. They've set up their boutique in the family room in the basement. They're known as the Knot Sisters. They had what they call a Pop-Up Sale in their boutique downstairs from 2:00-4:00 p.m. Folks stopped in and they even had refreshments to be enjoyed.

When everyone else had left, my younger grandson, Christian, returned with the two friends who had spent last night with him here at the house. Their teenage appetites were in full swing and my grandson was going to heat up some Pizza Rolls. "Would I like some?" He said he was going to use the microwave.

At this point, I was sitting in the living room. The area is open between the living room and the kitchen table where my grandson sat to devour a Nestle's Drumstick, to tide him over until the Pizza Rolls were ready.

The next thing I know I look through the pass-through into the kitchen and see smoke billowing forth. My 6'2", 260 lb, 15-year-old grandson was waving the hand towel to disperse the smoke and looks in at me and calls, "What do I do now?"

He hadn't used the microwave. He had used the big oven. I don't use my large oven much at all, but rely on my toaster oven and the microwave. Therefore, the large oven is handy for storage.

The items in the large oven this afternoon were a huge frying pan, at least two bags of granola, one large bag of tortilla chips, one package of saltines for chili, and an unopened box of Crispix. The yellow clip with the red lettering that had been on top of the tortilla chips has a totally new shape now.

Well, okay, not a lot of people store things in their oven, but I do. I guess I have since I've lived alone and don't use it much. The oven was a great solution as to what to do with the large fry pan, as it took up way too much room in one of the cabinets.

The other boys were alerted by the three smoke alarms, which were definitely working and indicating that smoke was present. We all sprang into action.

The laundry room door to the garage was opened and the double garage door. The two boys opened kitchen windows, which caused a cross breeze when the two dining room windows were opened. The front and back doors in the living room were opened, causing another cross breeze. The kitchen and living room ceiling fans were activated. My bedroom windows and the bathroom windows were opened. It was a typical Kansas day with the wind. So, airing out this place went pretty fast.

Thank the Lord smoke rises, because later when I went downstairs to the family room boutique, there was no aroma of smoke at all! The three teenage boys were sound asleep there. This was an evening when I enjoyed my deck.

About sundown, I called to the boys and said I was going for a walk. We'd clean out the oven when I got back.

When I returned, I noticed my grandson's car was gone. They were probably at one of the boys' homes trying to find something to take care of their ravenous appetites.

A phone call informed me that they'd be back in about five minutes and they were.

The bag of tortilla chips had burst and it would have been great to have my Dyson to clean up the myriad of crumbs!

At 10:00 o'clock, I sat down to finally eat some supper. The boys were at home and I was here by myself. The hall smoke alarm was binging every twenty-eight seconds (I timed it!) and I decided it wasn't going to stop. There's a magnet on my fridge that has the fire department's phone number on it, so I called it.

About 10:55 p.ml, as I sat trying to record all this in my journal, a knock came at the door and the fire chief entered. He located the sturdy stepstool out in the garage and, as I followed the fire chief carrying it through the living room, I noticed a larger red truck out front now with yellow or gold lettering.

Four firemen were headed toward my lighted porch. I told them I was so glad that they didn't arrive with their sirens ablare! One fireman stated that they try not to do it at night if they don't have to do so.

Did I have a nine-volt battery? A look at where I keep my battery supply revealed that there were plenty of AAs and AAAs, but no nine-volts.

The chief asked if there were any nine-volt batteries on the truck. There weren't. One of the firemen informed me that the batteries in the alarms should be changed when the clocks are changed in the spring and fall. I hadn't changed them.

The firemen left and the fire chief took my name, address, and phone number. He said he'd send a fireman over in the morning to put a battery in the hall smoke alarm to tide me over until I could get to a store if I was going to be home. I was!

About 12:15 a.m., I decided it was time to stop writing in my journal and close up shop around here. It was time to head for bed. I did leave one bedroom window open about two inches to continue to let fresh air into the house. Spraying Febreeze had helped.

When I woke up about 4:55 a.m. with the breeze blowing in my face, I made sure I was covered up warmly enough. As I lay there thinking over the events of the day, before going back to sleep, the moment when Christian stood in the middle of the kitchen floor waving the hand towel to try to disperse the smoke and looked at me and asked, "What do I do now, Grandma?" kept playing on my mind.

I don't know why, but it kept striking my funny bone and I'd burst out in a hearty laugh every time. There were a lot of hearty laughs over that moment!

As a couple of days have passed, two other moments have stuck out in my mind regarding this moment. I'd written this story and Christian read it. When he had a group over, they were given this story to read. He told them to be sure to read where it tells how he tried to burn his grandma's house down.

When they were all exiting through the front door, Christian was at the back of the group. He looked back at me with that heartwarming smile of his and said, "I'm really sorry about that fire, Grandma!"

The third part of this trilogy happened on Monday morning after the fireman had been here to install the nine-volt battery in the hall smoke detector.

I took the gallon of milk out of the fridge to put milk on my cereal. When I went to put it back, the shelf collapsed. I emptied out what food I needed to so I could try and put the shelf back. It soon became obvious to me that it wouldn't go back in the present condition. Both of the back hooks had been bent outwards.

I put the items from the top shelf on other shelves and shut the refrigerator door for the time being.

At least two more gallons of milk and I don't know what else had been put on that shelf (none to gently either, I might add) while the Pop-Up Sale was in progress at the boutique on Sunday afternoon.

It is now the evening of Tuesday, April 11th. The windows are open because of the beautiful weather we had today. The high for today was 70 degrees. Since the part for the Dyson has not been found, I'll have to order another part. Therefore, the stove has not been fully cleaned out at this point.

A neighbor couldn't find the part either, but he did fix the refrigerator shelf. Evidently, too much weight was put on the shelf Sunday afternoon. Most of the smoke aroma has dissipated.

This brings to close a trilogy of events that livened up those Golden Years!

ARTIST'S PROOF
Jan Zimmerman

Twilight falling

as trees shudder with the breath

of the evening breeze,

colors blend

as day turns into night once again.

Tentative footsteps

crawl and hop from beneath a bush,

nature has freed

the creatures of the night.

The owls hoot

their soulful sound…

up the ladders of the moon,

Rabbits feast on grass sweetened by the dew

and I…

I feast my eyes upon the beauty

of one more day as

twilight falls.

QUICK TRIP
Sherry A. Phillips

As I fling open the heavy walnut front door of the Desert Dragon Casino and find myself in an opium den, all I want is a restroom and a cup of black coffee.

The smoky dim atmosphere punctuated with neon splash gives me flashbacks. Rows of one-armed bandits are now amputees. I wonder how you get the game going. The loud rhythm of Bing, Ping, and Bong, Bong, Bong of the slot machines vibrate my hearing aids.

I hurry left, then right down another row past a cashier cage and a pop machine. Women. The familiar door swings into a spotless two-stall lavatory. I sit and none too soon. My bladder doesn't hold as much for as long as the days when I would zone out in labyrinths like the Desert Dragon.

I shiver and remember making my first bet. She was a roan named Kimberly Dawn at the race track in Denver. I was 13 and used three bucks from my allowance. The horse came in fourth, but I swore I would name my daughter after her. Now I chuckle and give thanks I birthed two sons.

Relieved and after scrubbing my hands, I hunt for coffee down rows of noisy neon. A couple of anorexic middle-age women in skinny jeans loll on high back stools, flip-flops hanging by toes. No laughter. No chit-chat. No fun. How could I have wasted eight years of my younger life feeding pennies, nickels, quarters then dollars into slots with voracious appetites? At least I could pull a handle. For a while it was fun. But addiction grows until you are consumed.

I find the free coffee and pour mine to go. After a year of rehab and 10 happy years of marriage, I can leave behind the chokehold that lurks here inside this heavy walnut door.

October air is frosty with promise. I take a sip of coffee, then turn to read the warning sign on the wall. "If you or someone you know has an addiction to gambling, call 1-800-672-4135."

*Note: This was originally written as a writing assignment about a fictional memory.

SOVEREIGN OF THE ENDLESS SKIES
R.E. Brown

Last evening

I chanced to look up and witness the majestic sovereign of the endless
skies,

the bald eagle,

dodging desperately through bare winter branches of the giant hackberry

hoping to evade my two spirit brothers;

raucous, harassing, impudent crows.

I,

distant cousin to Nezahualcoyotl,

gave thanks to the Great Spirit

for that Vision.

DEAR BILL...
Bonnie Lacey Krenning

Each year when Valentine's Day draws near, my mind goes back to remembering the many valentines my Bill and I shared in our many years of marriage and the two years we dated. We met when I was sixteen and we married when I was eighteen.

I soon learned that Bill loved giving and receiving greeting cards for holidays and special occasions—especially valentines. He saved all the cards our four kids and I gave him in the secretary desk that I gave him a few years after we were married, so he could keep his papers, bills and keepsakes organized and in order.

When we had been married several years, we had an especially difficult winter. The weather was extremely severe and bills were high. We had a skimpy Christmas. The kids didn't seem to notice, but Bill and I did. In addition, there was a lot of sickness: tonsillectomies, appendectomies and colds, just to name a few. Add to these problems—or maybe because of all the problems—Bill and I didn't agree on much, often arguing or not speaking at all to each other. I knew, however, that I loved him and he loved me.

As Valentine's Day approached, as always, I looked for a valentine for him. But they all seemed so glossy and phony, at least I thought Bill would think they were. So, one day while he was at work, I took a half sheet of white paper and a red ink pen and wrote a note in longhand, in non-rhyming poetry form. I titled it "Dear Bill, I Love You," stating how he was a good husband, a good father, always there for us, and other qualities he demonstrated.

On Valentine's Day, Bill was home for lunch, sitting quietly in his captain's chair, watching TV. The kids were at school. I laid the folded note I had written on the table beside his plate. He ate lunch, then left to go back to work. I didn't see him read the note. He didn't comment on it, but it disappeared from sight.

Later that afternoon, when he came home from work, he brought me the usual—or unusual—large, fancy, valentine-shaped box of expensive chocolates. He never said so, but I believe the reason he could afford such a large, expensive box of chocolates was that they were greatly discounted late on Valentine's Day. It didn't matter to me, because he, the kids and I had all the candy we wanted.

Then a few days later while looking in his desk for something, I saw the note I had written among his keepsakes.

With the coming of spring, we began working through our problems. We started appreciating and enjoying each other's company. I often noticed the note I wrote in his desk, but neither of us ever mentioned it.

With the passing of time, however, the continuing struggles, stresses and disappointments in life again caused frictions.

Then one day when I was at home alone at his desk, looking over the bills, wondering how we were going to pay them, I noticed the note I wrote again. On a sudden impulse, I jerked it out of the slot and ripped it into several pieces.

Bill never mentioned the missing note. I never mentioned it, but I'm sure he noticed.

Well, we finally grew up and became better at communicating and working through our problems. The whole family took many vacations, especially to Colorado. It didn't hurt that my brother had a horse ranch there. We also went to the Ozarks in Missouri, where Bill's parents lived.

Throughout this time there were many boxes of candy and many valentines exchanged. One valentine in particular stands out and I still have it. It reads: I'm so glad that in God's design He planned it so your path crossed mine.

I often thought of rewriting the note, expanding a little on it. After many years I did, but wasn't sure how or when to give it to him. Then the right time came! The small church Bill and I attended planned a Valentine Banquet for all the couples at a nearby restaurant in the banquet room.

At the same time, we had a women's Bible Study group that was discussing marriage relationships. I told them about the note and the history of it, and about not giving the rewritten version to Bill. I read it to them. They liked it and someone suggested that I read it to him at the couple's banquet. All agreed to keep it a secret, and the pastor agreed to go along with the plan and help us.

After the banquet meal and while everyone was still sitting, the pastor stood and said, "Bonnie has something to share with us."

I stood up behind Bill, who was still seated and read the newly written note. "Dear Bill...."

Bill sat quietly, as did all the others, for a long moment. Then the men started coming over to him, where he was still seated. They shook his hand, smiled and said he was making it hard for them to live up to him. I was so proud of him. I noticed his dimples deepen, which meant he was smiling on the inside.

After saying our goodbyes to all our friends in the banquet room, Bill helped me into my winter coat. Then we slipped out into the winter night, but we weren't bothered by the cold. The snow softly fell as we headed for home to enjoy the rest of the evening together.

Bill has been waiting for me in Heaven for over ten years. When the time comes, we will spend Eternity together, talking and agreeing on everything. Well, almost everything.

DEAR BILL, I LOVE YOU
Bonnie Lacey Krenning

Because you represent to me all that God expects a husband to be.

Because you are a wonderful, giving father to our children.

Because you are more concerned for me than you are for yourself.

Because you sometimes understand me better than I understand myself.

Because you are always there for me.

Because you encourage me in the things I try to do.

Because you are not afraid to tell me when I am wrong.

Because you like and accept me as I am.

Because you tolerate, even accept and love my family.

Because you were so good to my Mother.

Because you are my best friend.

Because of the secrets we share.

Because you love me.

Because you are God's gift to me.

Because you stopped, with my friends, and picked me up that Sunday afternoon on March 15th, so many years ago.

Love Always,
Bonnie

THE MESSENGER
E. L. Morrow

They believed they were the only people in the world. It was a reasonable belief. An earthquake blocked access to their small village centuries earlier. Surrounded by unscalable peaks on all sides, the people on the isolated plateau learned to adapt.

They depended on themselves and each other, lived in peace working for the benefit of all. They became self-sufficient. What they did not grow, catch or hunt they learned to do without. Much of their success can be attributed to their three leaders. Each leader served a particular function contributing to the common good.

One kept the traditions of the people. At the time we are remembering, Belinda was the keeper of the traditions. She held the memories of the people from the past and used her knowledge to benefit the people. Like the time when the children became ill because they did not have enough protein in their diets; she remembered a similar time when they had depended on rabbits for meat. When the rabbits became scarce, they switched to hunting squirrels. Now the same thing occurred with the squirrel populations. However, in the intervening decades rabbits had returned in sufficient numbers. So Belinda told the story, and they began to hunt rabbits again. The children had meat. Because they listened, disaster was averted.

A craftsman always served as another leader. He made tools and understood the use of leverage to increase strength. At the time we will remember, Matumba was the craftsman. One time while picking mushrooms, a child got trapped in a hollow under a fallen tree. The tree fell catching the child unaware and pinning her. Matumba realized they could tie some of their vine ropes around the downed tree. Using a nearby sturdy tree and leverage, they raised it enough to slide in another log freeing the child. Following his instructions averted disaster.

Diahanu was the third leader during this time: the problem solver. For example, when the stream normally providing their water dried up, Diahanu traveled up the dry riverbed until he reached a place where a rockslide blocked the stream. A recent earthquake caused the blockage diverting the water into another channel far from their homes. Diahanu determined they could remove enough of the rubble to allow water to flow again in its original channel. By listening to the problem solver, disaster was averted.

For many generations, they lived this way. Then one day a stranger, injured and hungry, showed up. They bandaged his cuts and gave him food, drink, and rest. He wore skins from animals none of the people ever saw, had a beard, and looked different.

Since they had never seen another person, the villagers assumed he was a Messenger from God. Actually, he was an incompetent soldier. Ordered to guide reinforcements to a fierce battle, he became disoriented by the fires set by the enemy along the route. After several days, he decided not to go home, because he would be stoned as a deserter. So he traveled higher in the mountains. He accidentally stumbled on a passage through the back of a cave, that led him into this isolated area, and eventually this village.

As he recovered, a significant problem became evident; they could not understand a word he spoke. The people treated him royally, built him a hut in the center. They gave him first pick of the food, and generally treated him with reverence. A plan began to form in his mind.

He began to teach them his language. They followed him around as he pointed to objects, giving his name for them. The people told him their names for the same things, but he didn't seem interested. Verbs were harder—distinguishing "go" from "run" required a lot of gestures and demonstrations. The people learned his every word because, after all, he was a messenger from God, and they did not want to miss the message.

After a few days, they had enough language to talk. Each evening they would gather at the central campfire, and the people spoke of their lives, traditions, and customs. The visitor was invited to speak, but he would only tell them about "… evil people who will come and destroy you." The people knew there were no other people, and none of them would harm another. In these evening discussions, the newcomer noticed how the people depended on the three leaders; sometimes for details of their stories. Other times the people sought their leaders help in interpreting his words to them.

The newcomer realized, I found this place; others can too. If others come, these people cannot defend themselves or me. So he taught the children to "fight" and "play war." He also usurped the toolmaker's skill, coercing him into making weapons: stone axes, spears, bows, and arrows. They also dug pits with sharp spears mounted in the bottom. Children who showed skill in fighting received honor, and those who did poorly were shamed. Many of the people did not like these changes—but he was God's messenger.

One evening he declared only his language could be spoken.

Belinda objected. "Our words are important to us. They convey our traditions, stories and values. They are the words our parents used to comfort us when we were frightened children. They are the words we learned when worshipping or celebrating. How can we learn from the past if we must always use different words?"

 The stranger, would-be-king, declared that the past is unimportant, and Belinda could only remain if she did not speak in public, and no one privately sought her advice. So the people used the new language. The change was not easy. He talked about things they never experienced, using words such as enemy, fear, hate, attack, and cowards. But his language also lacked words for love, respect, tenderness, compassion, or even God.

They did not like it, but he was a messenger sent to them.

***

"The Messenger," as the people now called him, had become the recognized authority. Yet people still turned to the problem solver for help. One evening he asked Diahanu, "Two young men, each want to mate the same young women. They cannot agree, so they come to you. How do you decide which one gets her?"

"That's easy. The woman chooses. The person most affected by something always decides. Then others accept and support the decision."

The people all nodded agreement.

Their new supreme leader immediately said, "Wrong. Women and girls have no choice. The men choose. From now on, women and girls must not speak in public. They may not go on hunts, play with boys, or learn to fight. They are to tend gardens, repair the huts, and have babies."

The people were dismayed.

But of Diahanu, he said, "Since he is so wrong, no one may ask his advice on anything."

The people did not like it, but they followed his instructions because he was The Messenger.

This went on for years. They prepared for an attack. Their King lived in luxury, while everything else fell apart. No one laughed, and everyone worked from sunup to sundown preparing for an invasion. They barely got time for the normal activities of hunting, gardening, feeding and caring for one another. The women and girls were required to help dig trenches and pits or replace the dried covering with fresh ones. Even Belinda and Diahanu were required to help with the "defenses," but no one could speak to them. If anyone used the old language, or talked to the old leaders, children were encouraged to spy on their parents and report to the King

Finally, the attack came. Not from an outside enemy, but from their own. Some of the youth who had trained most of their lives decided not to wait to be overrun but to go in search of the enemy. When their parents refused to join them, some young men pounced upon them while they slept. Several died. Others, including women and children, were injured.

Horror and disbelief followed. Some people said, "Has anything like this ever happened? We must ask Belinda." Then they remembered they were forbidden to speak with her.

They also remembered they had waited for The Messenger's words from God. "The only thing we ever received from him was about hate, killing, weapons, and disrespect for the old ways." They demanded he deliver his message.

He possessed no real message. So he landed in the prison constructed for his enemies.

They turned to the three traditional leaders, asking for their help. Their leaders first had to express their anger and hurt. They proclaimed their disappointment at how quickly the people abandoned the ways that had provided for them and their ancestors. Trust had been broken. The fabric of their collaborative, supportive community had been severely damaged.

The community met for a time of mourning. From their soul searching, they crafted a statement attempting to restore unity. "After the dead are honored, we must set about restoring order, and erasing the corrupting influence of the Stranger. Perhaps we have learned the difference between leadership and dominance. If so some good can be salvaged from our tragedy."

FROG RESCUING
Gwendolyn Eldridge Gandy

I hadn't had any luck finding a job for this summer. So, my mother posted my name on the information bulletin board at the grocery store. She thought it might be a good way to find something in our neighborhood.

I did get calls for house sitting, childcare, dog walking, and other household duties. It seemed that putting my name out there turned out to be a good move. I felt good about having jobs I could walk to and not take up more than five to six hours out of my day.

After the unbelievably horrible day that I had on this particular day, I decided to treat myself. I spent time in an upscale boutique shop called "Gigi's." I looked for an eye catching and dazzling swimsuit for the pool party that night. The only thing that caught my eyes were the high prices they charged for a few pieces of strings they called a swimsuit. The cost of those colorful strings was way more than I thought they should be. As the sales clerk made her way over to me, I told her I was just looking.

The money I had earned that day for babysitting that weird little beast, Bobby Bell, wasn't enough for just being in the same room with him. Caring for him should be another factor in the sale.

Bobby had stuffed his frog "Zipper" into a toy dump truck, only to realize that just one door opened and that none of the plastic windows would roll up or down. He couldn't get Zipper out. He started screaming and Zipper began flipping and flopping around as much as possible.

I went into a state of shock and panic. The clock had seemed to loudly tick and my heart pounded. I couldn't think. I knew time was running out for all of us. Somehow, I cracked the front windshield and broke through that hard plastic to free Zipper.

I need to add "frog rescuing" to my job skill set! But I will not do CPR on a frog, unless the frog turns into a prince!

When Bobby's mother came home, he was still looking for Zipper. Once freed the frog hopped away never to be seen again—if he was smart. I had thanked her, taken my money, and left.

I pulled in a sigh and forced back the memory of the day I had survived. I deserved that sparkling aqua blue and rose swimsuit, no matter the cost!

OH, SHENANDOAH
LoisAnn Seiwert

Oh, Shenandoah, I long to see you.
Oh, Shenandoah, I long to hear you.

'Tis six long years since last I saw you.
Oh, Shenandoah, I'm loved and left you.

Oh, Shenandoah, my heart it aches so.
Family and friends, ne'r to see again.

My dear and I fled by dark of night.
But now alone, I must seek our dream.

Oh, Shenandoah, I'm bound to travel.
For rivers flow and I must follow.

To seek my valley of abundance.
To make a home, to find contentment.

Oh, Shenandoah, your memory is so dear.
I hear your music singing.

Oh, Shenandoah, I see your valleys.
Their beauty will sustain me, as I cross the wide Missouri.

THE DREAM AND THE ROSE
Gerald McCoy

In a kingdom from which we are separated by both time and distance, there was a young peasant girl and her father who lived in a shack he built by a meadow. Her mother died in childbirth, and so her father raised her by himself.

As a small girl, she watched her father build their home with little material, but lots of love. Each day that he worked he told his daughter a story. He would tell her that he was building a strong and elegant castle, and that the meadow was a kingdom. He said that he would be the king and that she would be the princess, and the most beautiful girl in the land.

One day, her father promised her a handsome knight would surely ride across the meadow on a great stallion seeking to ask the king for the princess' hand in marriage.

But the meadow was in the shadow of a hill on which the real king's castle stood. As she grew up, the girl would sit in the meadow with her back to their shack and gaze at the castle. She grew sadder as time went by, for she realized that her father wasn't a king and the cottage wasn't a castle. She saw that she was a peasant, not a princess, and, of course, handsome knights on mighty stallions don't seek the hand of a peasant girl.

***

One summer night, the girl was lying on her cot looking out her bedroom window. A very bright and very full moon made the meadow look as if it had been covered with snow. She could clearly see the castle on the hill on the horizon. As she looked out the window, her eyes grew more and more tired until she fell asleep.

That night she dreamed she was the princess and the most beautiful girl in the land. She dreamed her father was the king and their shack was a castle. She dreamed she was walking in the meadow on an early autumn evening. It was just as her father had described it when she was a little girl.

As she was walking back to the castle, she began to hear the sound of horses on the run. She whirled and saw a band of seven evil knights riding fast and hard, charging straight toward her. She tried to run. She tried to scream, but she was frozen with fear. As the knights rode by, the leader pulled the princess onto his horse. They rode for the forest with the princess crying, the knights laughing, and at the castle, her father the king was heartbroken.

When they made their way into a ravine in the forest, the evil knight threw the princess to the ground as she begged for mercy.

"Please let me go." She sobbed. "I want to go back to my father at the castle."

But the men just laughed as she pleaded.

The laughter of the knights was replaced by silence as, one by one, each knight looked to the top of the ridge.

When the princess turned her eyes in that direction, she saw a single shining knight on a snorting white stallion. He was framed by two trees and his silver armor glowed in the moonlight. The frosty breath of the horse and rider could be seen in the cold night air. For all the world, he looked like a ghost, a paladin of God.

"Be gone, my friend!" The evil knight said with venom. "Be gone, or you'll taste my steel!"

The stallion began kicking and pawing at the ground with a great force, but the shining knight said nothing.

"Don't test me!" the evil knight shouted.

Without a word, the solitary knight drew his sword as the stallion began a furious descent down the wall of the ravine. Before the evil knights could regain their mounts, the bold knight had reached them. The princess watched the great battle that followed.

The rescuer was an expert swordsman. He deftly dodged their weapons. The battle was waged with the sound of thunder. Single handedly he fought the evil knights; each of their blows blocked by his sword. In turn, the silver knight struck his targets with deadly regularity.

Finally, the evil knight's followers had all been killed and only the evil knight remained. His rage was terrific; the fighting was fierce. Sparks flew as steel met steel.

With a loud curse, the evil knight took a mighty swing at the shining helmet.

The silver knight barely ducked the sword, but he countered with a thrust of his weapon. The sword caught the evil knight just under the ribs.

For a moment, there was no movement; there was no sound. Everything seemed to stop. The solitary knight withdrew his sword and the evil knight crumpled to the ground.

The knight sheathed his sword and walked to the princess. Gently, he scooped her into his arms and carried her to his horse. When he put her in the saddle, at once the spirited stallion became as docile as a mare.

Dawn's first light was shining when they returned to the castle. There was so much fear for the princess, no one in the kingdom had slept. A spontaneous celebration greeted their arrival, but throughout the ordeal, the knight had said not one word.

When the princess climbed down from the horse, servants led her to her private chambers and the king asked the knight for an account of the events. The knight told the king exactly what happened, and when he had finished giving his testimony, the king bowed before him.

"Sir, you have returned to me the thing I cherish most," the king proclaimed. "What I have means nothing to me compared to my daughter." The king paused and looked at the knight and said, "Name your reward—anything you like, even my very throne."

The crowd gasped at the king's words. But, as the knight began to speak, silence prevailed. "Your majesty, I have but one request. I would like one last look at your daughter before I continue my journey."

The king and the knight quietly slipped into the princess' bedroom. Exhausted from her adventure and relieved of her fears, she had fallen into a peaceful sleep. The early morning sun was shining through the window and the knight thought the princess was the most beautiful girl who ever lived.

During the trip back to the castle, the knight had fallen in love with the princess. But a knight who marries the daughter of a king should be the son of a king, for a man who marries the daughter of a king will one day be king himself. He knew he could never be the ruler of a kingdom, because he was just a common knight. He believed he would be a good husband, but he was afraid he'd be a bad king. That wouldn't have been fair for the people, and it wouldn't have been best for her. That was all the knight wanted. He wanted what was best for the princess no matter how much it hurt.

The knight knew that if a person really loves someone, he thinks of the other person first. It just wasn't in his heart to be selfish and satisfy his own desires at the expense of the princess' needs. He knew that one day, perhaps very soon, the right man would arrive. The right man could be both a husband to the princess and a ruler of the people.

The knight thought about those things and realized that, even though he loved her very much, he was not the right man for her. As he stood there watching her sleep, the knight could hear nothing, save the princess softly breathing and his own heart breaking. Then he knew that it was time to leave.

The knight didn't wish to disturb the princess, so he laid a single red rose on the beautiful, ornate night stand by her bed. This would be a symbol of his eternal devotion. The knight and the king quietly slipped out of the princess' quarters.

That morning, the knight left the kingdom, never to be seen again.

***

The peasant girl awoke as the morning sun shone brightly on a new day. For the very briefest of moments, she thought the dream had been real. But as she blinked her eyes, she saw she was looking through the same window through which she had been looking as she fell asleep the night before. She saw the meadow beyond the shack and the castle on the hill.

She knew then that it was all a dream. Alas, she wasn't really a princess. There had been no knight in shining armor.

As she looked out her window, she became very sad, sadder than words can ever say. She couldn't hold back a tear and it began to roll down her face. Then there was another, and another, and another. Soon she was crying as she had never cried before.

When she couldn't bear to look out the window any longer, she rolled over. As she did, she looked at the small wooden table that her father had so lovingly built for her. And there on that little table by her cot, what did she see through tear filled eyes?

A single red rose.

CODE 3 — A LITTLE INTRIGUE STORY
LoisAnn Seiwert

The gray late afternoon sky with thick mist caused Julie to take several minutes to gain her composure, and remember that she was no longer in Seattle. Adjusting her fingerprinting-proof gloves and glancing at the wall clock, she realized that she had slept for 12 hours. Upon checking the encryption decoder communicator, she saw no activity.

"No messages!" she exclaimed as she glanced out the window across the room. She went to the fridge to check for any food. Opening the package of graham crackers and a strawberry yogurt, she started remembering all the craziness of the last 24 hours.

He had been angry in a way that she had never seen before. "It's now 9:05 p.m. If you and all your stuff aren't out of here by midnight, you are dead meat! I'm not putting up with any more mess and bother in my space. I brought your CD player and TV up with me. I'm going to the basement where it's quiet—maybe I can get some sleep!"

Not more than two weeks ago she had finished creating three escape plans with a couple of friends who were concerned for her safety. With a little thought, she had readily agreed to the idea. She felt a wave of fear about what could have happened. She was thankful that they had pressured her about the matter.

As she remembered making the phone call last night, she shook. "This is Julie. I need an immediate Code 3 to remove all of me before midnight." She had been so afraid that he would change his mind or do something violent before she could get out of there.

The rest of the night was a blur. Loading her clothes and belongings into the old ice cream truck, the anxious journey down the dark winding back roads to the private airport, and phone calls at pay phone booths along the way. They had exchanged her cell phone for a private communication device that had a connection with them, if she needed to contact them during her escape journey.

Presently she couldn't remember what she had chosen to leave behind.

She could only recall parts of the flight. They had kindly roused her to warn that they were landing and it would probably be quite bumpy. By that time, she had a pounding headache and felt like she might vomit.

Landing and unloading cargo had been successful. She was left in this strange looking building hidden under rocks and vegetation, with a strict warning to read and heed all directions on the protocol sheet for survival in a hideout arrangement.

She got up to look out the window and saw only an open meadow in front. She realized that she couldn't even tell where the plane had landed. There seemed to be an old path that might have been a road at one time.

"Perhaps that's where they landed the plane." she mused as she began to consider the reality of her situation. She didn't know her whereabouts. She couldn't go outside, use lights or activate any electronic devices. She was supposed to be invisible until she heard from Code 3 with further instructions.

She sat down in a comfortable chair beneath a skylight and away from the window and the dreary weather outside. She had found a good mystery book to pass the time.

As her thoughts wandered, the question of an airplane landing strip became clear to her. Pin lights had been installed just below ground level, along the path in the meadow. She remembered them describing how they had installed mini solar panels in the nearby tree limbs and the lights were activated only by a wireless transmitter in the plane.

Suddenly a speaker mounted on the wall behind her crackled. She jumped, grabbing her communication device and the survival protocol. "This is Code 3 instructions: Connect at hour 22 pronto. Follow plan 7 for movement. Leave no trace of presence. Use provided bags for personal and discard. Destination has been arranged. Message repeats until coded response per protocol is received.

 "This is Code 3…

"Confirmation received. Landing hour 22 pronto."

***

As Julie (alias James Jones) settled into her train seat, she finally started to relax. This train thing seems to be working out ok. I just need to keep my voice strained. Or pretend to have a bad sore throat. There's nobody around me. It all should go quite well.

Then she opened the envelope they had handed her when they dropped her off at the train station. She found a ticket showing Chicago Grand Central Station. What happens after that?

As she read the instructions, she remembered the plan. They had reserved a room for James Jones at the Midtown Travelers Hostel just two blocks from the station. She was to maintain alias identity while she acquired any necessary wardrobe and accessories to be used in public, and until she found a suitable location to change her attire. The castoffs were to be left at homeless collection boxes, putting different pieces in different boxes.

Slowly reading the next part, she felt tears rising from the swirl of mixed emotions. "At hour 03, the Seattle address was assaulted by a L. A. affiliated hit squad to complete a retaliation mission. Occupant was asleep in the basement and did not survive an escape attempt. Our transmission informant indicated the completed mission. There were no questions of other personal involvement to create follow-up activity or surveillance. It appears that the Code 3 plans as executed were successful. You will hear from us soon. For now… Blessings and Good Luck!"

It took her several minutes to find her composure and remember that she had to maintain her alias persona. She had been overwhelmed with relief and awareness of the depth of the whole experience.

She finally remembered to read the rest of the instructions, which reminded her that the gloves and the instruction paperwork were all dissolvable in water using the included packet of activators. These instructions needed to be promptly accomplished to complete the Plan 7 mission.

So, she folded the letter, inserted it into its envelope and put them in the inside pocket of her denim jacket. Adjusting her leather gloves and cowboy hat, she was careful not to mess up her weathered suntan makeup. She reclined the coach seat and laid there listening to the clack of the train wheels on the track. Sometime later she fell asleep after marveling at the reality of people and events being different than they appear and how lucky and blessed she was at this time.

"We will be arriving into Chicago Grand Central Station in 45 minutes. If you are changing trains there, we need to see your ticket before you leave the train." The announcement jerked Julie awake.

Oh my! I must have slept for several hours. She stretched, trying to clear her brain. Sure am glad I woke enough to hear the conductor. So, my plan now is to find some food. A Chicago hot dog sounds really good. She blinked away the last of her fuzziness. Then I need to get settled in my room. Hopefully I can find a local map, that would be a big help for casing out the neighborhood.

The train station was crowded with travelers, and she noticed some young people in white robes milling around as she looked for a clock. It was almost two o'clock. She decided to take a different route to avoid the activity, something about how you could be saved from your sins. The hot dog she'd finally bought had really hit the spot, so she bought another one, a bottle of coke and a bag of chips to take with her for later.

She had put a small note pad in her jeans pocket just in case she needed it. And she had a pen in her inner jacket pocket so she could write down her room number when she got to the Hostel. At the desk, she pointed to her throat and handed the clerk the note asking for a room for James Jones. As she finished at the desk and headed for the elevator, she became aware of a couple of guys eyeing her. She looked straight ahead, relieved when the elevator door opened and they did not follow her.

When the door closed behind her in her room, she let out a huge sigh of relief.

Sitting in the recliner chair, Julie pulled out the local area map she had found at the train station. It would be a big help tomorrow when she made her journey to plot her plan of action.

She remembered the instructions to destroy the gloves and got up to complete that part of the plan. It was interesting to see the "leather" gloves dissolve and watch everything disappear down the drain. She could now use the medical gloves they had given her before she got on the train to keep her hands covered.

As she checked her makeup to make sure it was still in place, a raucous noise in the hallway startled her. Apparently, there were several guys out there carrying on, a couple of them sounded as if they were drunk and they were joshing with each other.

When she heard one of them going on about "that dude with the gloves and cowboy hat and what was that all about?", she felt anxious. I'd better go out real early in the morning to case things out. Hopefully those guys would be sleeping off their partying and it would be quieter and safer.

***

The sun was just rising as Julie went out into the streets with map in her hand. She had marked a few places that looked promising and she needed to find convenient drop off boxes. Luckily there were several in this part of the city. So that was not going to be a problem.

She turned to go down one of the alleys that she had marked on her map. It was a relief to see there wasn't much there except a couple of trash receptacles.

A turn into an intersecting alley proved more fruitful. She found what she had hoped for: a door inset into a building. Hardly anyone could see her there. When she came tomorrow, she could shed the alias outfit that she would have on over her own clothes. It would only take a few seconds to do that. Then she would change to her tennis shoes and put everything into her tote bag. She would then be good to go. She could empty the tote bag on her way to the 24-hr restaurant she had passed as she was checking the alleys.

A real breakfast with bacon, eggs and pancakes sounds really good, she thought as she headed back to the Hostel. She stopped at some vending machines outside a small grocery store that wasn't yet open. At least she could get a sandwich and a package of cookies to tide her over for the day. Perhaps she would go out later in the day for more food, but that was a scary idea.

There was no one in the lobby when she arrived. Seconds later, she heaved a sigh of relief as she entered her room. If she left very early in the morning, she must have everything ready. Including a note to leave with her key about hitting the road so there are no hang-ups to cause a problem.

She gathered her things together and planned exactly what she would wear under the alias outfit, and how she would carry her belongings with her. She decided that she could come back after breakfast and some window shopping, and then get a room as Julie Woods. At the train station, they had given her enough cash for a couple of days until they would meet again. That meant she could do that and get some real food to eat.

***

When she left the next morning, there was no one at the desk. Thankful, Julie left the key and note on the counter. She headed out into the early morning light.

The last step of this escape journey was completed pronto as she was on her way to have breakfast. She dropped first the shoes and cowboy hat in one box, the denim jacket in another, and the cowboy shirt and travel bag in yet another.

At the restaurant, she felt a wave of relief flow thru her as she waited for her eggs and pancakes. She decided to go to the Art Museum after she reserved herself a room at the Hostel. First though, she would do some window shopping to pass some time. She would also stop at the thrift store she had passed to see if there was anything she needed for herself. Perhaps her friends were in the area and they could meet her at the Museum.

As she walked back to the Hostel, she called them on her communication device. "This is Julie. Code 3 journey is complete. Am going to the Art Museum for the afternoon. Can meet you at 3 o'clock if you are in the area. Call me at 3 if you are not available so we can plan our next connections. Thanks so much for everything!"

DOWN BY THE RIVERSIDE
LoisAnn Seiwert

I'm gonna lay down my heavy load
Down by the riverside, down by the riverside, down by the riverside
I'm gonna take off my marching shoes
Down by the riverside, down by the riverside, down by the riverside
I ain't gonna study war no more.

I'm gonna put on my robe of peace
Down by the riverside, down by the riverside, down by the riverside
And wrap round my waist a sash of joy
Down by the riverside, down by the riverside, down by the riverside
I ain't gonna study war no more.

I'm gonna lace up my travelin' shoes
Down by the riverside, down by the riverside, down by the riverside
And walk on down to the River of Life
Down by the riverside, down by the riverside, down by the riverside
I ain't gonna study war no more.

I'm gonna walk with my brothers so wise
Down by the riverside, down by the riverside, down by the riverside
I'm gonna join with my sisters so strong
Down by the riverside, down by the riverside, down by the riverside
We ain't gonna study war no more.

And we'll all join hands with love and joy
Down by the riverside, down by the riverside, down by the riverside
And sing out loud and long and strong
Down by the riverside, down by the riverside, down by the riverside
That we ain't gonna study war no more.

You can repeat the last verse in a higher key with regard for emphasis, particularly with the last statement. Perhaps it could even be musically spoken with strong voices.

TURNING FIFTY IN A HORSE TANK
Cherise Langenberg

I have never been afraid of getting older. As a matter of fact, with my job as a Senior Center Director, I celebrate aging every day. I have people turning sixty, seventy, eighty, and ninety on a fairly regular basis. We have monthly birthday parties, "Hip" Hikers, and an Aging Gracefully series at our center. So, I am the "champion/cheerleader" for older folk—myself included.

I believe in "Re-firing"—not Retiring! (And I am so adamant about that wording, I am trademarking it!) I also hate the word "bucket list." Kick that bucket list notion to the curb. Start living now, not in the future. People should live on the improv. So, why did 50 years of living have to get my attention?

It must be the menopausal, dubious hot flashes, and incoherent brain slog that by age fifty captured my attention! I am not sure exactly why this has agitated me, as the major birthdays were zinging by at an astounding rate. I remember my "Sweet Sixteen," when I got my beautiful pearls. At eighteen, I was thrilled when I reached the voting age. The age of twenty-one was no big deal to me, as I am not a drinker. I always partied well without alcohol, and never desired to be drunk and out of control. If you knew me you would know that I have a hard time with the laughing gas at the dentist's office, so drinking does not appeal to me. I'd rather laugh without the gas than have someone control my laughter!

Thirty was a fun time—not, as I was in the middle of raising three little ones, homeschooling and trying to have a minute alone in the bathroom. I doubt if I had time to ponder aging at all.

Forty was identifiable, kind of like Haley's comet. There was a tail-like the sagging skin under my arms! At forty, Dave, one of my good friends, took a sabbatical to write a book and reminisce about being forty. Leslie was another friend who started her trek of running marathons. She recently ran the Pike's Peak Marathon, which I think is a death wish. I rather wonder where her desire to run came from, as she never ran before? Maybe it was Leslie's menopausal brain slog; it obviously started earlier than mine! But at forty I wasn't slowing down to even contemplate my navel. Of course, I couldn 't see mine, with the rate I was still moving at Haley's frenzied speed of 3600km an hour! Slow down, people suggested. "I am alright" was my polite answer. We were in the middle of running our business, running a home, taking care of the kiddos, and still trying to find time to breathe!

I think I started this mid-life crisis around the age of forty-five (I was always maturing earlier than my counterparts). I remember it quite well. I was at the American Society on Aging Conference, in Chicago, right on the "Magnificent Mile." In the middle of all the classes, thoughts, papers, theories and intellectual confines of aging, and after a full day of conferencing, I decided I would call my husband, Scott, and tell him I wanted a convertible! I wanted to cruise the "Magnificent Mile," and feel the wind in my hair—while I still had hair. I remember I put Scott on speaker phone to demand my request. He laughed and said "Yes"—I could have a convertible. I was surprised. He never said yes to spending money, as he was a dyed-in-the-wool accountant. So, it was good to have my co-workers listening in—as witnesses!

After I came home from Chicago, I drove a few different convertibles, and couldn't find one that could seat five people—aka the fam. I had to re-think that desire. I finally had figured that a sunroof would do the trick, but I needed one that was probably more of an SUV. So I could still haul the kiddos, who were growing at a rapid rate.

For my 25th anniversary gift—although we had been married twenty-eight years, we bought a Ford Flex. Yeah! I finally had the black/silver car to celebrate my 25th silver anniversary. It was super-exciting, and I was ready to cruise! So was my twelve-year-old daughter, and fifteen-year-old son!

I can remember getting in the car, after we purchased it. Seth, my middle son, wanted to navigate the blue tooth—and I was happy my teeth were still attached. My mini-me, Atiera, sat in the front seat with me. We both smiled from ear to ear, until I opened the sunroof to the bright sun of a May day, and started to back out from the car dealership. As I was looking in the rearview mirror, I gasped! My gorgeous silver anniversary vehicle was showing all of my silvery-white-gray hair off. I was speechless and horrified. I couldn't believe it. I always had chocolaty dark hair. With the natural sunlight, I looked as old as Methuselah! I looked directly at my daughter and said, "I didn't know I was turning so gray!" She laughed and said, "I thought you knew!" I immediately shut the sunroof and the extra door to shut all the sunlight out. Awk! It has still yet to be opened.

Okay, so after the "Shock and Awe" situation in the Flex, I decided to think about my motto for a healthy lifestyle: "Lose 50 by 50!" I wanted to try to lose 50 pounds. It would be a great accomplishment, but I really needed to have started about six months earlier. When I finally figured it out, I only had two months to take off 50 lbs. I hate to say it, but if it took me seventeen years to put on the extra hundred pounds, I think it may take me more than two months to remove my excess layers of added "loveablity." So, that motto, had to change as well, to "Lose 50 in 50 more years."

Alright, I addressed the material needs of turning fifty, and the physical needs of fifty. I was going nowhere fast. I decided to address the mental and spiritual aspects of turning fifty, as it was looming upon me. I felt as though I needed to take a trip and "get away." Some people say they need to "Find themselves," but I just needed to find a place to re-boot, relax and not have to serve someone dinner, entertain anyone, or provide service with a smile. What I wanted was actually selfish, but honestly, I have been helping people and children and my husband for many, many years—so I just wanted some time to myself.

In 2006, we went with my mother and my little kids in tow, to my great aunt's funeral in Scottsbluff, NE. After the service, we decided to go on up to see Mount Rushmore and the Crazy Horse Monuments. It was a great trip. On the way back, we hit a lot of National Monuments, including the Badlands—beautiful at sunset—and then went through Valentine, NE. I loved Valentine and the stunning beauty of the Sandhills—the great secret of the Heartland. The Sandhills are a cross between the Flinthills and Sand dunes. It makes me think of the Flinthills, but on a smaller scale, as the sand dunes make smaller hills to view. The vault of blue sky over the land is amazing when you are in the Sandhills. The clouds and sky are stunning during storms and when the sun is rising and setting. I always feel a release in my spirit when I see the sky and the brilliant views our Lord has given us!

The amazing thing about Valentine, is Fort Niobrara National Wildlife Refuge. This is an amazing place. It is where the East meets the West, and the North meets the South. We have the Deciduous forest meets the Coniferous forest and where the Short Grass and Tall Grass Prairies meet. The numerous flora and different types of fauna are so varied that it makes this area one of the most unique places in the world. The Niobrara is the only National scenic waterway/byway in America today. Not to mention the variety of birds and animals this wilderness supports. So, when we travelled through, I made a commitment to myself to return and "float" down the Niobrara River.

So, this is where the river meets the highway. I needed an escape. I loaded the car with my camping gear: the tent, flashlight, sleeping bags, the snacks, water, hiking gear, bug spray, sunscreen, floppy hat, shades, and swimsuit. Then I decided at the last minute to take my chaperone. My eighteen-year-old son, Asa. He would be a great chaperone, as he was going through some of his own life changes. He had recently graduated from high school and was to start college shortly. I told him it would be a great chance to get away and have some fun with his fifty-year-old mom. But the crux of the matter was that he was a certified first aide life guard, and I might need one during our great adventure.

Off we went, certainly not with the sunroof open, but we were armed and ready to enjoy the adventure of a lifetime! I didn't want to see another person, at least not anyone I knew. That way I wouldn't have to be cook, chief, bottle washer, entertainer, or hostess with the mostest! I would be free! I wanted quiet, sand hills, marsh lands, ponds, cattle and windmills, and blue skies to boot.

We got on the highway and headed North. We got through Broken Bow, NE and we started to hear the deafening noise of the Harley Davidson motorcycles, as they passed us on the two-lane highway. It kind of scared the bejeezers out of us. We would be trekking peacefully along and then zoom, along came a leather clad person, with the bandana waving behind. I was appalled. I wanted peacefulness, and yet it didn't come! Finally, we stopped for gas and we found out Sturgis was happening in South Dakota, so the cyclists were on their way to their promised land.

We finally stopped for the night and stayed in the Nebraska National Forest. And, yes, I know what you are thinking: Does Nebraska really have a forest? The answer is yes! The forest was planted early in the 21st century when people were needing jobs.

Asa and I got there about sunset, and had to put the tent up in the near-darkness. I thought we got a great deal, as we got a campsite for $8 a night! It seemed like a great bargain until the train whistles started blowing. Every 45 minutes, I swear—and I may have every time a train came through. It echoed, and the noise from the highway and train bounced over the river and through the woods to Cherise's tent we go! Asa and I had, needless to say, a challenging time sleeping that evening. It actually may have taken another year off my life—or added another one!

Early the next am, my chaperone and I were scheduled to get to the river for our float trip extraordinaire. It was a Friday morning, and I wanted to float the river, and hopefully, see no one else. We got to the drop-off site just in time to miss the driver! So, we had to hitch a ride with another float crew. We decided to float the "non-party" part of the river. This is the part of the river that is in the National Park—the part where no alcohol is allowed. The last several miles are not in the National park, so those that partake in the spirits, are in their element!

When we got to the river, we put the horse tank in the water! We had a table in the middle, and folding chairs to boot. We had a cooler, with beer. Ooops rootbeer, that is, and sandwiches and chips. This was the life, rednecking on the Niobrara. We made sure our phones were secure in the waterproof bags, and then off we went with a push, floppy hat and all.

The water was about three-four feet deep and it kept us flying for four hours. During that time, we saw numerous birds: from Hawks to woodpeckers to Bald Eagles. We saw cows grazing on the National Forest land and playfully acknowledged them with friendly "Moos." My son did well navigating the tank, except when the Daddy Longlegs startled him and he yelled to high heaven! I almost had to slap the lifeguard, as he was about to go "Cow tipping" with his mother!

As we rounded each curve of the river, we saw a new vista, and the weather was perfect. Eighty degrees with blue skies, puffy clouds and no Harleys or trains. Actually, we saw no people throughout the trip. I had to do nothing except "be" in the moment, let the sun soak into my skin, and enjoy the birds' melodies as we passed them on the river. My spiritual side was renewed by this trip, as I passed the time in a quiet solitude with my son. We talked when needed, and yet had a camaraderie that fostered a quiet passing with the gurgling of the river.

The Lord answered my prayer, as we saw not a single soul on the river. It reminded me of how it may have been two hundred years ago with the Native American tribes that looked to the land to guide them, and they looked to the land to revive their souls. They were not all tied up in time constraints, schedules and over burdening of one's soul. They lived to see the sun rise and set. They only took from the land what they needed, and it provided that sustenance and shelter for them. They didn't care if they were fifty or five. They just lived.

So, my trip down the Niobrara was worth every penny and encumbrance. It was a one-of-a-kind trip. It renewed my spirit and rejuvenated my step. I want to encourage you to get an eighteen-year-old chaperone and horse tank and see where life leads you!

WATCH ME, DADDY!
A tribute to fathers
Nancy Breth

I am in Corpus Christi, a long weekend to spend time with my son Marty, his wife Holly, and grandson Albert. We are at one of Marty's favorite fishing spots spending the day fishing, wading and splashing in the water, and just relaxing together.

"Watch me, Daddy," Albert yells.

Albert has been learning to swim, really swim—not just the dog paddle, stay afloat kind of swimming that he had learned to do in his backyard pool. He has been practicing his swimming for a long time now and today feels ready to swim to the little island across the stream from where we are.

Albert begins his first attempt to swim all by himself across the stream. First, he yells, "Watch me, Daddy," and Marty drops everything he's doing and gives his full attention to his son.

As Albert pulls his arms in and out of the water and kicks furiously to stay on top of the water, Marty stays close enough behind that Albert can see him at every turn of his head. Marty keeps walking behind, close enough to see anything unexpected, to be there quickly if his son needs some help, but far enough away to let Albert know he trusts his strength and his faith in himself enough to let him go it alone.

He pays attention to Albert's every move and cheers him on offering up his guidance. "A little more to the right, son. You're getting off track. There you go. You can do it; you can do it. Yes! You did it!"

And we are all applauding.

As Albert stands up on the shore at the same place he took off, Marty says with pride in his voice, "Good job, son. Good job. All that hard work you did practicing was worth it, wasn't it?"

I can feel the glow of joy that is reflected in Albert's smile as he says, "Yes, Dad."

Every time we are together I am in awe of my son the father. Such an amazing transformation from boy to man to father is this child of mine. This boy who wanted to be so many things when he grew up—so many dreams he hoped for, tried out, but never really found that one great thing to be and do…until he fell in love with this woman and this child.

Not many boys say they want to grow up to be a father; but what greater purpose in life could there be for any man than to be a father and to teach their children what a real man is; what real love is. Watching over the children, cheering and steering them on, and always being there to make sure they don't get off their course. When they do, gently picking them up and pushing them on to keep working at being the best they can be, and applauding them for doing their best even when they fail.

And though they are taken for granted most of their lives, a father keeps on staying close at hand so he can always be there when his children yell out, "Watch me, Daddy!"

THE BRIDGE CLUB LADIES GO CAMPING

Gwendolyn Eldridge Gandy

This trip was for those who were on the brink of an older age, only in numbers not in ability. The group of lively ladies were clever, creative and adventuresome.

***

I had just finished high school and begun looking for a job. My aunt offered me a chance to earn a car, if I would chaperone her and her friend on a trip. How could I resist?

This would be my first real camping trip since I had been an eight-year-old Girl Scout. I was a little unsure of what would need to be packed for a camping trip. The ladies that I would travel with had been well-seasoned campers. They were looking forward to having a lot of fun on this trip.

Oh, should I mention that they were all over eighty years old?

As I mentioned, my Aunt Carrie roped me into being a chaperone/helper for this big adventure by promising me her old VW when I went off to college that fall. She had also assured me that this would be a trip of a life time.

***

On that first memorable day, we found our seats on the bus. Even that wasn't as easy as it seemed. Some complained about the sunlight; it was too bright on the windows. The seats weren't comfortable and there wasn't enough leg room. The list went on. I wondered if the VW was worth losing my sanity on the trip.

I had hoped that the women remembered what was needed for a camping trip…besides make-up cases, wigs, hair rollers, and some of the brightest red nail polish I had ever seen.

Helen had been smart enough to take a count of the ladies, and purchased boxes for Ensure, bottled water, denture cream, and cards. I was glad I hadn't forgotten my camera.

Somehow our first day hadn't been so bad. Except that Mary packed her hair spray instead of bug spray. So, the ants ate our food, and flies ate us. Carol burnt the popcorn. And Sue forgot to tie the canoe to the dock as we sat around the campfire that evening and sang songs.

The sky had been blue earlier; the moon shone brightly that night. We all agreed it was a fun day. Oh yes, Kay let us use her nose spray to fight off the mosquitos.

I couldn't wait to see what happened the next day.

A DAY ON THE TRAIN

Jan Zimmerman

Slivers of sunlight
slowly peeping through misty shadows,
Cigarettes shared in the darkness of half-dawn….
Words shared and memories traded
another day has started.

Feelings transposed from one to another
attitudes change like the ebb of a tide,
Grown-ups being childish
as children mature…
One road behind
a thousand more to go.

Dust of the road
a million hoofbeats strong
Chanting a rhythm of yesteryear….
Internal challenges of a magnitude untold
watching as each life unfolds.

Close to some
yet with a distance that won't be breached,
Should there be walls
or bridges by now.

Emptying the reservoir of my soul
till there is nothing left….
Going the extra mile
to be kicked harder
and trodden upon more often,
Is survival a key
or handicap?

Translucent skies over the many states
as people's true self emerge
more apparent each day.

THE TUG-OF-WAR
Another Pig Tale as told by Sophie
Jan Koelsch

Hi, my name is Sophie. My home is in Wichita, Kansas. I am a pot-belly pig. Most pigs live on a farm with lots of friends like cows, chickens, horses, and other critters. When I was just a wee little thing, a family was visiting the farm where I lived. They fell in love with me because I was just so cute. The family took me home that day to be loved and fed. Donna was the mom of the family. She was born blind. She has never seen the grass, the trees, the faces of her family or her friends, or me. She knew I was the perfect pig to take home. I learned not seeing meant Donna could do a lot of things in her own way. She had a good memory about things I did in my own home. She also understood I needed to go back to the farm to see my friends. She knew I missed them. One thing Donna did not know about me. I tell stories and like to call the stories Sophie's Pig Tales.

Stories are my way of helping animals learn about people, the way people live and how they treat each other. Just like animals, people are not alike. Some are big. Some are small. Other pigs come in different colors. People also have ways that make them special. There are people who have challenges that make them who they are. They are called people with disabilities.

A person with disabilities may be someone who cannot hear or see. A girl or boy may have trouble walking and use a wheelchair or something called a cane. There are people who are a little slow in thinking but can do what everyone else can do. A person with disabilities may need help from an animal called a service dog. Telling my stories help not only my animal friends to know it is okay to be who they are. My stories also make it easier for boys and girls to understand it is alright to be who they are. Each of us is special in our own way. I hope big people will learn these things, too.

All my friends are animals. Each one has things about them that make he/she unique. Let me introduce them to you. Callie Cow is one of my newest friends. Callie has beautiful brown eyes and is very nice. She likes everyone and does not know others can also be not so nice.

Stubby Dog is a fifteen-year-old small dog called a Schnauzer. Stubby does not hear too well. His eyes see really well. He tries to help his pal, Bristol. Bristol and Stubby have been friends for a long time.

Bristol Chimp is fun and onery. Bristol is also blind. Often Stubby will see for Bristol. Bristol will hear for Stubby. Friends help each other like that.

Denver Duck was in an accident one day. He was taking a nap in tall grass by a pond. The farmer came through with his mower and did not see Denver Duck. Denver Duck's foot and leg were cut off by the mower. The farmer took Denver to the vet. The vet was able to make a special foot and leg for Denver so he could walk and swim.

Then there is Shelby Sheep. Shelby is shy. She looks out for her friends, especially Denver Duck. Shelby is so shy she has a hard time talking to people. Her words sometime come out funny. It just takes the words time to come out.

I have a secret to tell you. Are you ready? Only my friends can hear my Pig Tales. This is the magical part of the group. Anyone can read my Pig Tales, but only my friends hear my stories. The stories help us understand people.

This is a true story about Donna, my family mom, and me. Donna does the grocery shopping. She knows I love, love, love apples. Rich, red, big, juicy apples. The kind of apples that just melt in your mouth with the first bite to the last bite.

Donna does not drive a car because she cannot see. So, when she goes to the grocery store, she has to take the bus. The bus driver comes to our house; helps her find a seat on the bus. After shopping, Donna rides the bus home. The bus driver is a nice man. He walks her to the front door. When she gets home, a neighbor comes over to help her put things away.

The last time Donna came home from the store, I could smell those apples and could see where the neighbor put the apples in the refrigerator. The only thing left was to decide when I was going to get one or more apples. If Donna decided, I knew only one apple was going to be my snack. If I decided, more than one apple was to be my snack. I just had to wait for the right time.

The neighbor finished putting the apples and the food away. She patted my head and told me to be a good girl. She was such a nice lady, so helpful. As she left, the phone rang. Donna went into the living room to answer the phone. The time couldn't be more perfect. I had to work fast.

Donna didn't realize her son taught me to open the refrigerator door with my nose. What a good kid! He was not home, so it was up to me if I wanted an apple. No more waiting for Sophie. No more being patient. It was time for one or more juicy apples to be in my mouth.

I looked around to see if Donna was still talking on the phone. She was so involved in talking to her friend, she didn't notice I had walked into the kitchen and opened the fridge door. There were my bright, shiny red apples, just waiting for me! Drat! The apples were in a bag, which meant it would take more time to get one. I could do it. Nothing was going to stop me.

All my attention was getting to the apples. I was so busy getting the bag open I didn't hear Donna sneak up on me.

"Sophie!" she said loudly in her mom voice, "What do you think you are doing!" By this time Donna was down on her hands and knees. She felt around for the bag in my mouth. "Sophie, give me those apples."

Donna couldn't see where I was, so I started to move away from her with the bag of apples in my mouth. Her grip on the bag was just as strong as my grip. A tug-of-war like no one had ever seen became the battle of the day. I pulled one way while Donna pulled another.

It did not take long for the bag to split open and apples went rolling in every direction across the floor. What a great thing for me! I put as many apples in my mouth as I could while trying to get in Donna's way from getting any.

Donna's son came home about that time. He realized what was going on and started to laugh. He tried to help Donna pick up apples, but it was just too funny.

"Are you two having a good time?" he asked.

"Well, Sophie certainly is," Donna chuckled. "She knows how to combine eating and exercising. Oh, by the way, since you taught her how to open the door to the refrigerator, you get to clean up her mess-apple cores and all."

"Ah, Mom," replied her son, "Sophie was only doing what she knows to do—eat, play and be funny!"

"I suppose you are right," Donna sighed. "Well, Sophie, this is a story that will make you famous. Just wait-my friends at work will hear about you."

I really didn't care who heard about me. All I wanted was more apples. People say an apple a day keeps the doctor away. I wonder if that is true for pigs as well as people. If it is, I'll be healthy for a long time.

The apples found a new home on the top shelf in the refrigerator. What Donna and her son and the neighbor don't know is there are bunches of ways to get apples. I just haven't learned all the ways, but I will. Apples really speak to me.

MONSTER ROSE
Another Pig Tale as told by Sophie
Jan Koelsch

Sophie was visiting the farm. Seeing her friends was always fun. I can hardly wait for my friends to see my new tank top. Her new tank top was awesome! It had stripes of yellow and green. The yellow was the color of Mt. Dew and the darker stripes were the color of grass. On the front was a huge green frog sitting on a lily pad. She looked so pretty.

She had a great story to tell them today. If she didn't hurry, her friends wouldn't get to hear it. She had taken time to eat an apple before putting on her tank top. "Everyone will wonder where I'm at," she said to herself as she moved her short legs.

All her friends were gathered at the pond. They cheered when they saw her.

"Sophie is here! Sophie is here!" Callie Cow yelled out. "Sophie is here everyone!" She loved Sophie so much. Sophie was such a good friend to her. She took time to explain things to Callie when no one else would. She missed Sophie not being at the farm.

Sophie just grinned. She had the best friends in the world. She was certain they would be her friends forever. She was really strutting her stuff, ready to show off her new tank top.

"Sssssssophie you look so pretty in your nnnnnnnnnnew tank tttttttttttttop. I lllllllllllllllove it," Shelby Sheep managed to spit out. It was hard for her to speak, but she knew Sophie would understand.

"Thanks, Shelby. It is a new top. Donna thought it would be something I would like," said Sophie, as she nodded in Shelby's direction. "Do you like the frog?"

Shelby, Callie and Denver Duck shook their heads with a big yes.

"That frog is so big it looks like it is going to jump off that lily pad straight into the pond," Stubby Dog whispered to Bristol Chimp. "Takes up the whole front of the tank top."

Bristol didn't exactly know what Stubby meant, but could only imagine a frog that large. "It is okay, Stubby. As long as Sophie likes it, that is good. I just want to hear her story. She does have a story to tell us, doesn't she?"

"Yes, I have a story to tell you. I can hear you," Sophie assured Bristol and Stubby.

With a look of getting caught, Stubby said, "Well, let's hear it." He hoped the story would take attention from himself.

Sophie began. "My story is about an old black 1970s truck Donna's hubby used to race. The truck was fondly named Monster Rose. Monster Rose had been the best in truck racing. She was unbeatable! There was a huge, hot pink rose painted on the hood. Rose sported a 427, V-8 engine that roared like a lion when she took off at the starting line. Twelve-inch racing slick tires gave her extra speed. Extra weight in her short bed gave much needed traction. The truck was fierce.

"My Donna's hubby would drive Monster Rose to every race possible. He always looked so handsome in his racing gear. His black helmet also sported a huge, hot pink rose that matched the rose on Monster Rose's hood. His driving gloves, jacket and shoes were black with the hot pink rose. They made a great looking, unforgettable pair!" Sophie felt so proud it seemed the green frog on her tank top got bigger as her chest swelled.

"There were many other trucks in the races. There was Big Mac, the 1960s bright red truck. The company that paid the bills for Big Mac was MacDougal's, makers of the best hamburgers. Big Mac had been around in many races for many years. Big Mac gave Monster Rose a good race, but always came in second. His driver never once thought Big Mac would not beat Monster Rose. It didn't seem to matter how much his driver pushed Big Mac. Big Mac would be maybe five seconds behind Monster Rose. Monster Rose's driver often wondered if hamburger grease would make Big Mac run quicker.

"Awesome Arnie was another big truck to give Monster Rose a run for her money. Awesome Arnie was the newest of all the trucks. He was a handsome royal blue with a pewter finish. His driver considered

Awesome Arnie to be the coolest looking truck in all racing. Awesome Arnie also like Monster Rose had a 427, V-8 engine. The engine had been changed so the noise level was quiet and powerful. Awesome Arnie came in third behind Monster Rose in most every race.

"Bruiser Bob was the loudest truck in all racing. His driver was a big guy as well. He bragged to the other drivers that good and big were better than looks. Winning was the only thing that mattered to Bruiser Bob's driver. He felt looks didn't win races. Bruiser Bob had seen better days. The truck was very dusty and had lots of dents from taking some corners too fast. Everyone wondered how many more races there were for Bruiser Bob and his driver.

"These four were the best in the racing field. Other trucks were no match. Fans of truck racing could expect the best race when each was at the starting line. Fans also were aware that each truck was going to be in the top four. They knew Monster Rose and her driver were the best."

Sophie paused, and then smiled as she looked at her friends. Each one was leaning forward as if they were waiting for another race to begin.

"The last race for Monster Rose and her driver would be the best race of all time-the Grand National Championship," Sophie explained.

All at the same time, Sophie's friends shouted, "Why was this the last race for Monster Rose? That was not fair to Monster Rose!"

Sophie put it in plain words. "Monster Rose's driver knew her better than anyone else. He recognized Monster Rose had just enough energy and drive to win. He wanted Monster Rose to be remembered as the greatest truck ever. The Grand National Championship happened once in a lifetime. To win this race meant Monster Rose would always be the best. Monster Rose had set the bar high." As Sophie told about what the race meant, her friends were nodding their heads in understanding. Monster Rose just had to win this race.

Sophie remembered the day of the race just like it was yesterday. She wanted her friends to feel like they were there. Sophie walked closer to the group as she told more. "The weather was perfect the day of The Grand National Championship. Fans filled the stadium to overflowing. There was a lot of energy and excitement in the air. The people selling popcorn, peanuts, hotdogs, and sodas could not keep up with the fans' calls for the food."

"Wow, Sophie! I can't wait to hear more. What a great story to hear today," said Denver Duck, bobbing up and down in the pond. "I feel like I am right there!"

Sophie kept going, pleased to hear Denver's comment. "Monster Rose had been washed, polished and was dazzling in the sunlight. The hot pink rose was more brilliant than any other time in her racing history. She was fine. Her tires were aired to the exact amount needed. Her gas tank was full of the best fuel possible. Everything was perfect.

"The conditions of the track were great. Each truck has qualified in many trials for this race. Starting time was fast approaching. Only one winner would be Grand National Champion. The trucks would complete ten laps without an accident and the best time. Whichever one crossed the finish line first would win.

"The announcement over the loud speaker said, 'All trucks to the starting line, please.'

"As Monster Rose's driver climbed into the seat, he put on his helmet and goggles. He adjusted the mirrors and his seat belt. He started the engine. Monster Rose purred. She was ready. Her driver revved the engine, put the truck in drive. He and Monster Rose were on their way to win the race.

"Big Mac, Awesome Arnie, and Bruiser Bob were already at the starting line. There were more trucks but none others mattered. The rules stated all trucks were to turn off their engines. Each was given a fair chance. Now it was time to wait for the announcer.

"'Ladies and gentlemen, boys and girls, all trucks and drivers, welcome to the Grand National Championship Race. Please stand and remove your hats for the national anthem.' As the music of the national anthem swept across the stadium, it was a proud moment. Monster Rose and her driver looked amazing.

"The crowd cheered after the music stopped and then it became very quiet. 'Drivers return to your trucks. You may start your engines.' The sound of engines being revved and the smell of the fuel filled the air.

"The crowd waited. The drivers were ready. The flag that signaled the start of the race was in the air. 'On your mark. Get set. Go!' The black and white checkered flag dropped! It was show time!

"Monster Rose took off and never looked back. Monster Rose's driver skillfully drove the course, making every curve with such precision. There had never been a more perfect race. By the time Monster Rose crossed the finish line, Bruiser Bob, Awesome Arnie and Big Mac still had another lap to finish. This had not been a competition. It had been Monster Rose's finest moment. It truly was a glory day for Monster Rose."

Sophie paused with a tear in her eye and pride in her voice. Her friends were so absorbed in the story they did not even realize it was done.

It didn't take long for her friends to begin cheering. "Yeah for Monster Rose! Yeah for her driver! What a race!" they all called out.

"Oh, Sophie, that was an amazing story," said Bristol. "I could actually see everything. I felt like I was actually there."

"Thanks, Bristol. That is what I hoped for," Sophie proclaimed. "Monster Rose will always be the best and always be National Grand Champion."

"Hurrah for Monster Rose!" her friends yelled.

Sophie stayed and visited a bit longer, and then it was time to go home.

"Do you have to go, Sophie?" Callie asked. "Another story would be nice."

"There will be other days I'll come visit and other stories to tell. See you all later."

Sophie began the long walk for her short legs to the front gate. Ah, I love being a story teller. My Pig Tales will be in my friends' hearts forever.

Monster Rose will be Grand National Champ, too.

GOING TO TOWN
Another Pig Tale as told by Sophie
Jan Koelsch

Sophie Pig needed to go to the grocery store. She was out of apples. Apples—large, juicy red apples. Apples were one of her favorite foods. Her mouth watered as she thought about apples. Her mom, Donna, was at work so it would be a while before she could get apples for Sophie. Sophie could go get the apples herself, but that really was not a good idea. "What can I do?" she asked herself.

Time for a nap. That is what I'll do. I'll take a nap. Maybe by the time I wake up, Donna will be home. She can go get the apples for me. Sophie jumped up on the sofa in her favorite spot. Before long, she was deep in sleep.

The time passed quickly and Donna was home. "Well, hello, my Sophie," she softly said as she stroked Sophie's head. She wanted to wake Sophie up, but did not want to scare her.

Sophie so liked having her head stroked, she snuggled down more.

"Sophie, you just keep sleeping. I'll tell you later about a little boy who came to my job today. It is quite a good story."

Sophie heard the word story and her eyes popped open. She loved a good story. She knew her friends would, too. She managed to jump down from the sofa and waddle behind Donna to the kitchen. Donna might also have apples. There were no apples, but Donna had started fixing lunch. That was good, too.

Donna felt Sophie's wet nose against her leg. "So, I guess you do want to hear about the little boy who came to my job today," she giggled.

Sophie nuzzled Donna's leg as if to say "You bet."

Donna works at a place that helps people with important things. She told Sophie a ten-year-old little boy came to her job. His name was Oscar. He was using a wheelchair. She explained, "He had a disease called MD. MD keeps his legs from moving or holding him up. It also keeps him from walking and running. He would fall down without his wheelchair. The wheelchair helps him to get to places like a grocery store or playground.

"It was a beautiful day with the sun shining with a gentle breeze blowing. It was a perfect day to go to town and get some things he wanted. Oscar had asked his friend, Elmer, to go with him. Elmer was busy and couldn't go. Elmer usually went everywhere with him. He helped Oscar by pushing the wheelchair. Elmer's mom decided he had chores to do. Oscar understood that. Moms could be that way. So, he had decided to try to push himself and go to town. He knew after a short time he just couldn't do it. He had to get help. When he got to Donna's job, he knew he could get help there.

"Oscar asked Donna if there was someone there who could help him. He explained what had happened and how hard it was to push himself. His arms just were not that strong. He became very tired. Was there anyone that could help push him back home?

"Oscar told her crossing the street at the corners was especially tough. Not every corner had a curb cut. A curb cut is a place at the corner that is cut out to make a ramp. The ramp makes it easy to cross the street if a person is in a wheelchair or has a hard time stepping down off a curb. The curb cut is good for everyone. 'If there is not a curb cut at every corner,' Oscar explained, 'he had to go down the street until he found a curb cut.' He had worn himself out."

As Sophie listened to the story, she wondered why if curb cuts were good for everyone, why weren't curb cuts at every corner. Then people who were in wheelchairs or had trouble stepping off curbs would have an easier time crossing the street. She thought it would be easier for her to cross the street if there were curb cuts. It wasn't exactly easy for her to step down off the curb. She had four legs and her plump body to move. She liked walking down the ramp rather than stepping off the curb. Once her two front feet had missed the step off the curb. She went tumbling head over heels. She had hurt her back and had spent a lot of time on the couch. Walking down a ramp was a great idea.

Donna noticed Sophie had a thoughtful look on her face. She knew Sophie well enough to know she was not listening. "Guess maybe I should make a grocery list," Donna commented. "I'll make sure apples are at the top of the list."

Apples? Had Donna said apples? Sophie decided maybe she should be paying attention to the story about Oscar. After all, she was the storyteller and had to remember every detail to tell her friends. She grunted to Donna.

Donna chuckled. She knew what Sophie liked. She also knew how important it was to tell Oscar's story.

"Donna's friend, Steve, pushed Oscar home. It was ten long blocks and on the other side of the street to Oscar's house. Steve told Donna when he came back that there were no curb cuts anywhere. He was tired after pushing Oscar all that way and then walking back. He could only imagine how hard it was for Oscar."

Sophie thought, "Steve is such a hero to help Oscar get home." She was not aware there was more to the story.

Donna continued. "Steve and I feel there should be curb cuts on every street corner. Just think, Sophie, I can't see the curb. I would fall if there wasn't a curb cut."

Sophie knew that would not be good. If Donna fell, she could hurt her ankle or her foot. She wouldn't be able to go get apples for her! She realized how big a problem this was.

"Steve has a plan to help Oscar and everyone. He is going to the next city council meeting to tell those people how curb cuts help everyone," Donna said. "He wants Oscar to go to the meeting with him. Just think, Sophie. Oscar could be the hero for lots of people. If he had not come to my job today, no one would know about what makes it easier for him." Donna was clapping her hands. "Isn't that a good story, Sophie? Everyone wins."

Well, not everyone, Sophie pondered. I still don't have my apples. But I do have a new story for my friends. I guess that is a win.

THE REAL STORY OF CINDERELLA
Another Sophie's Pig Tale
Jan Koelsch

Sophie the Pig was looking around the barnyard. It was a hot, humid day with temperatures in the 90s. "Wow." she said, as a trickle of sweat dripped down her rosy, round check. She wondered where everyone was today. They were all probably down by the pond, either standing in the water or soaking up the coolness of the water. The shade from the big, old oak tree overshadowed the pond, keeping the water from absorbing too much heat from the sun.

She decided she would waddle down to the pond. She enjoyed seeing her friends and telling them stories. She had a really great story to tell them today.

Sure enough as the pond came into view, Sophie saw all her friends there. Denver Duck was happily swimming. With his new special leg and foot made by the nice vet, he was able to paddle around the pond from one end to the other. His new special leg and foot helped him a bunch. Callie Cow was standing in the water looking very contented. She had those beautiful brown eyes of hers closed. She told him there just wasn't anything better than standing in cool water on a hot, humid day.

Denver splashed water at Callie, getting her wet all over. Her eyes suddenly opened in surprise, wondering what had happened. He had already quickly paddled away, hoping she wouldn't see him. She shook the water off and closed her eyes.

Sophie chuckled at Denver Duck's mischief.

Sophie noticed Bristle the Chimp sitting in an old, leftover tire swing. That swing had been there for many years. It hung down from one of the larger tree branches. Kids in past summers would come down to the pond, using the tire swing as a diving board or just to swing. Some even used the tire swing to sit while throwing fishing lines into the pond.

Bristle felt some of the water from Denver splashing Callie, but she couldn't see what the commotion was about. That was okay, Bristle thought. You don't have to see to enjoy swinging.

Stubby the Schnauzer Dog saw the whole thing between Denver and Callie. He just chuckled. Even though he couldn't hear much being said, he knew things were okay. Bristle was okay, too. So, things were good. He was just enjoying watching out for everyone. He saw Shelby Sheep standing in the shallow end of the pond. She was also munching the green grass at the edge of the pond. "Enjoying that grass, Shelby?" asked Stubby.

Shelby was enjoying the grass so much she was not paying attention to her friends. Stubby's question had startled her. "Wwwwwhat?" she asked.

Stubby couldn't quite hear her answer, she spoke so softly.

Bristle heard the question. "Stubby wants to know if you are enjoying the grass, Shelby."

"Oooooh. Yesssssss I am," she said.

Bristle said to Stubby, "Shelby says she is enjoying the grass."

"That's good," said Stubby, as he lay in the cool grass. Just then he caught sight of Sophie. "Hey, Sophie. Hot enough for you today?"

"Stubby, it is hot and humid. Wish I was a hippopotamus," Sophie said with a smile. "Hippopotamuses like swimming under the water, as well as standing in the water. That is why they are called Sea Horses."

"I didn't know that. Can you ride them like a horse?" Stubby asked.

"I do not know, but I don't think so. You can't get a saddle around them," chuckled Sophie.

"Hey, gang, I have a story to tell you. Want to hear it?" Sophie yelled.

Everyone's ears perked up. They all turned their heads toward Sophie as she found a comfortable place in the mud to stand. The mud was cool and wet. For her, the mud and telling stories made the afternoon perfect. She loved telling stories to her friends. They were good listeners and always paid attention.

"This is a fairy tale about Cinderella. You all remember her, don't you? Cinderella had been happy until her mother died. Then after a while her father married a woman who had two daughters. The woman became Cinderella's step-mother."

"Yeah, and the step-mother was very mean and unkind to Cinderella," Denver said, as he helped Sophie tell the story.

"That is so right," said Sophie. "Anyway, the mean step-mother made Cinderella do all the chores. She had to wash the clothes and hang them out to dry. She had to scrub the floors. She also had to cook the meals and clean up the kitchen. Her step-mother made her move from the bedroom she loved to a room on the third floor that was very small. The room had one window. It had very little heat in the winter. She was not happy there but with her father gone so much, there was very little she could do. When her father was home, the mean, step-mother took all his time and attention."

Callie spoke up. "What made the step-mother mean? Why didn't she like Cinderella?"

"No one knows, Callie. Maybe someone had done something mean to her sometime. What do you all think?" Sophie looked around at the group. "Any ideas?"

No one had much to say. She waited and waited. Everyone had puzzled looks on their faces.

"'The step-mother's name was Esmerelda. One morning Esmerelda yelled for Cinderella to bring her coffee and breakfast. 'I'm coming as fast as I can,' Cinderella cried.

"'Hurry up, girl!' Esmerelda snarled.

"'You are so slow.'

"'I'm sorry', Cinderella offered. 'I try.'

"Cinderella had wondered why her step-mother treated her so mean. She knew how being mean toward her made her feel. It hurt her feelings. It made her wish she could run away. She tried not to cry. It was hard. She took a deep breath. She just had to know.

"'Step-mother, I want to ask you a question.'

"'What! You want to ask me a question? How dare you!' Esmerelda sneered.

"Cinderella knew she should probably say she was sorry for wanting to ask a question. She knew that Esmerelda might decide to hit her. She just had to know why her step-mother was so mean to her.

"'Step-mother, it is a small question. It won't take long to answer. Please!'

"'What is your question and make it fast. You have lots to do.' Esmerelda scoffed.

"Cinderella gulped and said, 'I try to do my best. It doesn't seem to make you happy. Why are you so mean to me?'

"Esmerelda did not like Cinderella's question. Her face was turning red. The question was a surprise to her. She did not like surprises. She waited for a short time before answering the question.

"'Cinderella, I do not have to answer your question. You really do not need to know. I will answer your question, if it will get you out of my room and back to your chores.'

"Cinderella waited. She had no idea what the answer would be. Her knees and legs were shaking. The waiting seemed like a very long time.

"Esmerelda said, 'Cinderella, when I was a young girl, I was very happy. I had a mother and a father who loved me. We were a family. One day when I was outside playing in the yard, a man in a shiny, red racecar drove up in front of our house. As he got out of his car, I noticed he was dressed in blue jeans and a yellow shirt. He was wearing white sports shoes. One shoe had a purple toe. He didn't say hello to me. He just walked up to the house and knocked on the door. My dad let the man in the house. Pretty soon I heard lots of yelling between the man and my dad. I was getting scared. My dad never used a loud voice.'

Sophie looked around at her friends and noticed they were listening, hardly moving a muscle.

Stubby said, "Keep going, Sophie, please. Why were Esmerelda's father and the man yelling?"

Sophie continued, "Esmerelda looked at Cinderella. 'Do you want to know what the fight was about, Cinderella?'

"All Cinderella could do was to shake her head. She couldn't move she was so scared.

"'The fight between my father and the man was about my mother. The man had come to take my mother away from my father and me. My mother, after a time, married the man. He became my step-father. He was mean to me. He made me do chores I did not want to do. He would not let me see my dad. He would lock me in my room.'

"Esmerelda was not looking at Cinderella. She was looking away. To Esmerelda it seemed like only yesterday when the man took her mother away in the racecar. That day was the last time she ever saw her father.

"Esmerelda looked at Cinderella with a very evil look. 'That day I decided that I would never be nice to anyone. My feelings were hurt. I missed my father. I could not see my mother. My step-father would not let her come into my room not even once. When I married your father, I decided to make you have the same life as I had. I did not like you and I wanted to make sure you knew it.'

"Cinderella was stunned. Esmerelda had answered her question. She certainly had. It was not the answer she had hoped for.

"Esmerelda stared at Cinderella. 'You aren't a bad girl. You just happen to live here. I do not like doing chores and I do not ever want my daughters to do chores. Those are your jobs. So, stop wasting my time and get back to work.'

"Cinderella just stood there. She was not sure what to do. She blurted out, 'That's just not fair. I just want you to know I do like you even if you are mean to me.' She quickly turned around and left the room.

"'Stupid girl,' Esmerelda muttered under her breath. 'She'll feel the same way some day. Then she will understand.'

"She took a sip of coffee. It was cold. 'Cinderella! My coffee is cold!'

"Cinderella shook her head, as she made her way back to Esmerelda's room. Some things will never change, she thought. She didn't dare say anything out loud. One day I will move from here. I will not treat anyone like Esmerelda has treated me. People are to be liked, not to be made feel bad.

"Cinderella met a nice prince and lived happily ever after. She was one of the nicest people ever. She knew how it felt when someone is mean. She also knew it was better to help people feel good."

Sophie quietly waited to see what her friends would say.

Many minutes passed before Bristle spoke up. "I hope none of you or I ever feel bad like that. I feel sorry for Esmerelda. It is too bad her step-father wasn't more kind. Then she could have been happy. She might not have treated Cinderella so bad."

Everyone agreed.

Denver Duck said, "I'm glad that is just a fairy tale and doesn't happen here."

"Me, too," said everyone else as one voice.

Sophie knew it was a fairy tale, a story. She also knew somewhere, some step-mother or step-father was being mean to a child. Somewhere a child was being mean to another child. She was just glad it wasn't that way with her friends.

It wasn't long before the group was back to enjoying the pond. Sophie was thinking about the pond and what stories it could tell. Another day, another day, she thought.

HAIKU GRANDMA
Connie Holt

A Haiku poem has three lines, and the first and last lines have five syllables each, while the middle line has seven syllables. They rarely rhyme, and they give the reader an immediate image.

Cool baby green grass
Gently cushions between toes.
Finally, spring has sprung!

Grandchildren around
Hiphopping ipods sounding—
Drowning out my voice.

Guardian Angel
Frets when I'm driving my car
Ready to rescue!

Dining at café
Egg on face and on my blouse
Becoming my mother.

Brooke observes the world—
She is not a girly girl.
Hope for science yet!

Kiara's sweet smile—
Honey-colored granddaughter—
Swiftly steals my heart.

ONE WAY TO SOLVE A PROBLEM
Sherry A. Phillips

"What's wrong, Robbie? Trouble with homework? Anything you need my help with?"

"Yes, yes, yes."

"If an Oreo and milk won't spoil your supper, we can tackle your challenge in the kitchen."

"I like the way you think, Mom."

The package rattled as she got him some cookies. She heard him glubbing milk.

"Okay, what's the big problem?"

"Well, you know, like, we've been studying family history…heritage, stuff like that."

"Darn, I thought this might be an English assignment."

"We have to write a paper about how our parents met."

"Oh, well, why don't you ask your dad?"

"He said to ask you."

"He did, eh? Then we better have another cookie."

"I'm thirteen and you and Dad have never told Serena and me about when you met."

"Robbie, it began at 2:00 am Tuesday, February 9th. My apartment on Riverdale Drive was on the second floor and every night about 1:30 am the new guy in the apartment above mine would turn on his surround sound to the overnight all music Latin station. The booming tempo woke me and the dead. After three nights of this, I knew we had to make a new arrangement."

"What did you do, Mom?"

"I marched right upstairs and banged on the door. And banged, then banged again. This new guy finely ripped open the door. Dripping wet, holding a towel around his waist. 'Did I interrupt your shower?' I shouted above the too loud salsa."

"I can't hear you. Let me turn the music down."

"Good, thanks. I'm sorry I interrupted, but I can't sleep when your music comes on so loud at 2 am."

"Can we talk about this next week? I'm on split shift at the hospital and want to keep alert. Got to get back at 4 am."

"Okay, Robbie, I need to start supper. Take your dad an Oreo and ask him to tell you the rest of the story."

Note: This was originally written as a dialogue assignment in a class and it was decided to leave it in this style.

MIKEY'S NEW FRIEND
Ptrice and Friends

"Hi, Mom, I'm home. What's there to eat?"

"I'm in here, Mikey. Come have a sandwich and milk, and tell me all about your day," Mom Tater said with a smile.

"Ah, Mom," her son groaned and walked into the kitchen. "You always want to know how my day went! It's only school!"

"You know, if I didn't love you, I wouldn't care how your day went. So, come on—humor me—I really do want to know about your day." She looked at him gently.

"Oh, we learned some new spelling words and some other things." He hesitated. "Mom, I met a new friend named Marty. I sort of asked him over for lunch Saturday. Is that okay? He's been sick a lot and I told him that I'd have to okay it with you and Dad."

She studied him in concern, saw the eagerness in his eyes. "Well, Mikey, we'll have to see. What kind of illness does Marty have?"

He looked worried. "Oh, the school nurse said he has AIDS, but for us kids not to worry. We couldn't catch it by just being around him."

This news really shook her up for a minute, but she said, "Mikey, let me see if Dad has any plans for Saturday. I'll let you know after school tomorrow night. That will still give you a couple of days to let Marty know."

All kinds of things started running through her head. Was it really safe? Should Mikey even be playing with a boy with that horrible disease? She wondered what Dad would say or think. Would he even allow Marty in the house?

That night after dinner she, Dad, Mikey and his three sisters, Krissy, Roni, and Andi all sat in a circle to have family devotions before heading off to bed. Afterward, she and Dad went in to kiss and tuck each of their children in for the night. As she leaned over to kiss Mikey goodnight, he whispered, "Don't forget to ask Dad about Saturday."

"Yes, dear, I won't forget." She smiled down at him. "Now, you have a good night's rest and we'll talk tomorrow."

She and Dad went back into the living room to settle in their favorite easy chairs to visit for a while. Then they would have their own private devotions before going to bed. She didn't quite know how to bring up the subject about Marty. Any type of major decision was always discussed before giving an answer. She decided the best way was to just say it.

"You know, hon, Mikey met a new friend at school this week. He wants to have him over for lunch and to play on Saturday. I told him that I needed to check with you first, to make sure that you didn't have any plans." She took a second before adding, "Also to make sure it was okay for Marty to come over."

He gazed at her curiously. "Well, I don't see any problems. I don't have anything planned until later in the evening. What's Marty like?"

"Mikey says he's a nice boy and he's real quiet."

"Boy, that would be a welcome relief, as rowdy and loud as Mikey and most of his friends are!" He must have noticed the concern on her face and asked, "What's wrong? Is he sick or something?"

She sighed. "Yes, dear, he is sick or something." She gathered her thoughts before explaining. "He has AIDS, but the school nurse told the children that it is okay to play with Marty. She said that they can't get what he has from just being around him." She was still worried, but she also felt sorry for the boy. "It sounds like he's kind of lonesome and maybe really needs a friend."

She met her husband's eyes. "You know, dear, we've always told the children to be friends, and not to treat people mean just because they are different."

He nodded, his brow furrowed in concern. "But, honey, is it really safe? Especially for him to eat here. Isn't it possible to catch it from him with us eating off the same plates and silverware?"

Uncertainty filled her. "I really don't know. We do have a dishwasher and it's supposed to make everything safe. I'll call the school nurse tomorrow and ask her about how we could catch it, and if there are some precautions we need to take."

"God knows all about this sort of thing. I think we should pray and ask His guidance on this," he said with confidence. "You should probably still talk to the school nurse. That way we can get more information about this disease."

The next day she called the school nurse, Miss Kelly. Miss Kelly explained that there were only three ways of catching AIDS: through blood contact and blood transfusions, which was how Marty Scallopine contacted the disease, through sexual relationships, and through a nursing mother's milk, if she was infected with the virus. The nurse also said that it was important to be careful around anyone that was bleeding. It was best to always wear rubber gloves when touching someone else's blood, and remove those rubber gloves by pulling them over themselves wrong sides out and disposing of them afterward. She explained that the disease could get into our systems through any open sore, like nicks or cuts on hands. And it was important to wash our hands with soap and water.

From what Mom Tater had learned, she agreed that there really wasn't any way children could pass it on to each other. And that it couldn't be passed on to her family using the dishes, when washed properly.

That night when Mikey got home his first question was, "Mom, can Marty come over Saturday?"

Confident with what she now understood, she said, "Yes, dear, Daddy and I talked it over and there's nothing planned. Now, let's plan what you're going to do with your new friend. Maybe you can even help fix some of the food." She gave him a loving smile.

"Great, Mom. What can I do?" His eyes lit with excitement.

"Okay, Mikey, what do you guys want to eat? Does Marty have a favorite food? Are there certain foods that he can't eat?"

He shrugged. "I don't know. I'll ask him tomorrow. Can we have a picnic?"

"Yes, a picnic might be kind of nice. I'll send a note with you to give to Marty for his mother so that she will know it's okay with us, and not just something that you guys have cooked up. I'll put our phone number on it so that she can let me know about the foods that he can eat."

She gook a second to think. "How does hamburgers, hot dogs, chips, beans, soft drinks, and cookies sound, if they're okay for him to eat? Friday night I'll fix some cookie dough. Then when you and the girls get home from school, you can cut out the cookies and decorate them. How's that?"

When he grinned in agreement, she asked, "Now, have you figured out what you and Marty want to do?"

"Well, Mom, I don't know if he'll feel up to playing football with Dad and me, so what do you think of playing table games? That way we could all play together. Everyone could get to know Marty, since he's real quiet and doesn't have many friends."

He looked sad. "Some of the other kids say that their parents don't want them to play with him because they're afraid he will make them sick. Mom, he even cries sometimes and Mrs. Butterworth has to take him out of class." Now his eyes filled with worry. "If I'm Marty's friend, will I get sick and die too? They say he could die."

Mom went over and put her arms around Mikey. "No, honey, just being Marty's friend is not going to make you or anyone else sick. Not everyone dies from AIDS. Most people do, but you know God is still in the miracle healing business."

She gave him a hug and he hugged her back. "Remember Jamie who helps in the children's programs at church? He had AIDS and God healed him. God can do it for Marty, too. It's all up to God and the plans He has for Marty's life. We'll just have to get serious with God and ask Him to touch Marty and heal him, too."

As he seemed hopeful, she added gently, "We must remember, though, God sometimes doesn't always heal a person here on earth. Sometimes that has to wait until they get to heaven. He may have that in mind for Marty, but it won't hurt to get busy and start praying every day for him and leave the timing to God."

She saw understanding in his gaze, along with some sadness. "Your other school mate's parents are just scared that something will happen to their young ones. They just don't know the facts. There is hardly any way you or your friends can catch AIDS by being Marty's friend. He wants a friend, and that's probably what makes him cry. Is Marty friendly?"

"Oh, yes, Mom." He bobbed his head. "And he says that he loves God, too."

"Well, then Marty does have at least one friend, Jesus." She smiled at her son. "In Proverbs 19:24, it tells us how to be a good friend There are friends who pretend to be friends, but there is a friend who sticks closer than a brother. Then in Proverbs 27:10, God's word tells us to hang on to those friends and not to desert them. It sounds like Marty needs one of those good friends that the Bible tells us about and not a pretend friend.

He looked serious. "Yeah, Mom. Would you pray with me for Marty and for God to help me be a good friend?"

"Yes," she said, proud of him. "Dear God, we know you love all your children, and in your word, you tell us that everywhere Jesus went He healed all that were sick. You also tell us to pray for each other. God, we're asking you to touch Marty and heal him. Lord, we thank you for taking care of him. We also ask you to help each of us to be real friends to Marty. Amen."

Friday while the children were in school, Mom Tater made the cookie dough and set it in the refrigerator to chill so that it would be ready for Mikey and the girls when they got home from school.

By the time the children got home, she had the board floured, rolling pin, cookie cutters, frosting and all kinds of decorations set out on the kitchen table ready to go. Mikey and Roni rolled out the dough, being careful to keep enough flour on the dough and rolling pin…as well as all over themselves. As soon as they cut out the cookies, Krissy slid a spatula under them and put them on the cookie sheet. She also put decorations on part of them and the rest they'd ice and decorate after they had baked.

With Krissy's help, she then put them in the oven and set the timer. Andi wanted to do something, but there wasn't much she could do. So, she snitched a chunk of cookie dough and hid under the table to eat it.

Soon all the cookies were done and decorated with each of the children getting one or two to eat. Even Andi got to put a few sprinkles and other decorations on some of the cookies, so everyone had a chance to help.

Saturday morning, Marty's mother brought him over and thanked them for allowing Mikey to be friends with Marty. Their friendship had made a difference in his spirit and he even seemed to be feeling better. The news made Mom Tater feel good.

Mikey hollered at Marty to come over to where he'd set out some games on the picnic table and introduced Marty to his sisters. They decided on a game that looked like fun for them all.

Meanwhile, Mom Tater invited Mrs. Scallopine to sit for a bit and visit. She wanted to discuss with her just what activities were safe for the boys to participate in, that would be safe for Marty. Mrs. Scallopine said at this stage of the disease, he could do most anything, but that he sometimes got tired easily. He knew what he could and could not do. She thanked Mom Tater again, and said that she needed to get back home. She would be back around 2 PM so that Marty could get an afternoon rest.

When the children had just finished their first game, Dad Tater asked if they wanted to play a little catch before they had to get the food on the grill. Marty squealed with joy. He told them that his dad had to work a lot and hardly ever got to play ball with him. So, Dad Tater got a bat and hit them some grounders. He was happy to watch the boys enjoying themselves.

While he was busy with the boys, Mom and the girls went in to start getting the hamburgers and the rest of the food ready.

After a while, Dad noticed that Marty was slowing down a bit. He decided that it was time to get the charcoal going if they ever wanted to eat. He invited Marty to come over and see how to start the charcoal. Marty looked surprised.

Mikey ran to get some newspaper and twigs to start the grill.

Next, they made a little mound of charcoal on top on the newspapers and twigs, and sprinkled it with lighter fluid. Dad told the guys that they should let the fluid soak into the charcoal, and then in a few minutes they'd light it. He cautioned them never to light the fire by themselves because sometimes the flame could flare up causing them to get burned badly. In a little bit, he showed them how to carefully light the fire with a long stick. When the mound of charcoal started turn white, he spread out the coals a bit and put the meat on to cook.

Marty piped up, "Boy, that's neat. I've never even gotten to help build a fire. Now I can tell my dad that I know how to start a fire and maybe he'll let me help him."

The boy's pleasure in being allowed to help made Dad happy that he'd taken the extra effort with him.

Soon lunch was ready. After grace was said, they all dug in. It seemed as though Mikey and Marty raced to see who could eat the most. Dad watched in amusement, thinking it was unbelievable the amount of food they put away.

After lunch Mom and the girls cleared away the food and dishes while Dad and the boys put out another game to play, before it was time for Marty to go.

Dad disappeared into the house and reappeared holding something red and blue in his hand "Marty, since you seem to like playing ball so much, how would you like one of our team's little league bats? I have an extra. Maybe next year when they have sign up times for our little league teams, you can join our team."

Marty was so happy tears welled up in his eyes.

"Oh, thank you. I always wanted to be on a little league team. Now I can be just like you, Mikey!" He ran over and hugged Mr. Tater's knees and Mikey's neck.

Dad felt touched, too, by the boy's delight. It was so neat to see such a sweet little guy so happy.

They all felt like they'd just been given warm fuzzies, but that's a different story.

Rolled Cookie Recipe

1 ½ cups flour

¼ tsp. baking power

¼ tsp. soda

¼ tsp. nutmeg

½ cup butter

1 egg

½ cup sugar

½ tsp. vanilla extract

½ tsp. grated lemon peel

Combine flour, baking powder, soda, and nutmeg. Cut in butter until mixture resembles coarse crumbs. Set aside.

In another mixing bowl, beat egg and add sugar gradually, beating well. Stir in vanilla and lemon peel. Blend egg mixture into flour mixture, mix to form dough.

Cover and chill in refrigerator for at least an hour.

Roll dough out onto a lightly floured board to about ¼ inch thickness. Cut out cookies with a floured cookie cutter. Place on lightly greased cookie sheet.

Bake at 375 degrees for 6 to 8 minutes. Cool and decorate as desired.

Yield: about 18 large cookies.

THE TATER FAMILY'S PURPOSE
Ptrice Collins

The purpose behind the Tater Family is to show others the family unit as God planned it. When the father is the head of the home and a major decision is to be made, the issue is discussed and an answer is given. My aim is to portray a family unit that loves together.

The Tater family's stories came about as an idea from our oldest granddaughter, Kristina, when she was 10. I had designed a collection of burlap dolls and among them there was a baby which she thought looked like a small potato, so she called it a "tater baby." By just playing around with some old nylon stockings, we did a little soft-sculpture and had some "tater babies." They naturally needed some family members to go with them. Before we knew it the Tater family was born.

It was Kristina's idea for us to write stories to go with the sets of dolls. I wasn't sure where to start or how to go about writing a story. So, I let it drop for a while. Until I again felt God nudging me to do something about writing.

I argued with God said, "I can't; I'm not qualified." I've never written a story! I don't have any training! I'm too old to start something new.

Finally, I felt God telling me in my spirit to start with children's books. Again, I asked, "But what would I write about?"

The thought came to me: What about the Taters? I'd forgotten all about them. Within fifteen minutes God had given me a half page of different ideas. You'd have thought that I'd have gotten the message by then. But I was so afraid of failure that I let a lot of things detour me. I didn't seem to have any time to do the things that I needed to do for my family, and I couldn't take off time from work.

A few days later, I had a bad fall at work injuring my back and both knees. Now, that's a hard way to learn a lesson and I don't recommend it to anyone else.

That Sunday during our church service there was a message that caused a quickening in my spirit, as if it was for me. I told one of the pastors what I thought God wanted me to do and how ill-equipped I felt.

He said, "God doesn't always call the equipped, but He always equips the call."

With the backing of three prayer partners, I sat down and started my first story. When I thought I had it finished, I gave a copy to each of the prayer partners and one to my son.

He informed me that the story wasn't finished yet. "You could add two or three more pages on this ending."

I prayed. Then I wound up with knee surgery. While in the hospital, God gave me a new ending. A few days later the news came out that Magic Johnson had been diagnosed with AIDS. I felt that maybe the timing was right for this story. I believed that God guided me on it.

Parts of this story are true. Mark (Marty) was a very close friend of our family. He contacted AIDS from a blood transfusion and died about a year after this story was written. This story was an attempt to help children dealing with the death of someone they've prayed to be healed.

SISTERS
Barbara Cairns

Once there were two little girls, sisters. Merry was just like her name: beautiful joyous, happy, and never fearful of new things. Barbara was similar to Merry in looks but was quite different in temperament. She was very timid and quiet.

As young children, the two girls were constant companions, playing together, amusing one another, champions to the other during outside disagreements, and comforting each other during illnesses.

Merry, the older of the two, would fight for her little sister, whether Barbara felt it was needed or not—and it usually was not. Merry didn't like that Barbara preferred dealing with her minor problems with quiet submission. Barbara was embarrassed by Merry's two-fisted attitude about every small transgression against either of them. But they loved one another and accepted their differences.

One of the differences between the two girls was their health. One was very healthy, only a cold now and then. The other had something hidden, something that only reared its ugly head occasionally and was very difficult to detect. You would think that Merry, the fighter, would be the one with great health. She certainly looked like she was healthy, just a little plump, rosy cheeks, clear complexion, but she was not. It seemed minor. You don't hear about it during holidays, with celebrities asking for donations, or on late night TV showing the young victims. Mother didn't even find out what it was after repeated visits to the doctor. Merry's illness must have been in her head, nothing showed up on tests or x-rays. There just wasn't anything wrong with her.

But, mother would sit with Merry, when her glands would swell while running a low-grade fever. She would have her drink plenty of water and get plenty of rest. She tried different diet changes, made sure she got plenty of vitamins and minerals, never knowing the cause and definitely not the cure.

This became common place. Merry never seemed too ill, just once in a while when she would have an episode. The thing was, however, the episodes affected her. When she would get a cold, to her it was more than just a cold. If there were new viruses, she would know she had that. This, this, whatever she had, was turning her into a hypochondriac. She had her bouts of true illnesses, and then she had the illnesses that she thought she had.

This in turn, changed Barbara—changed me. Instead of being understanding about Merry's illnesses, I became somewhat cynical. Why couldn't Merry just stop thinking she was so ill? Why did she have to learn to read so she would be able to check out her symptoms on the internet? Why couldn't she just be well?

When we were in our early twenties, I became ill. My chest and arm hurt. It was hard for me to breathe, but, as I usually did, I hoped the pain would subside and I would finally start feeling better. My mother noticed that I wasn't acting my usual self and asked about it. I confessed my pain and was a little worried about my heart. She shared that she had been feeling the same way. We decided it must have been some virus going around. Merry, too, was not feeling well. She had the same symptoms and insisted we take her to the immediate care. We did, and waited in the car. As we sat there, we saw so many people leaving with their arm in a sling. When Merry came out with her arm in a sling, we could not keep from laughing. She was incensed, accusing us of being uncaring. However, she could not stop our laughter.

A few days later, the news reported that a virus had hit our city, sending many to the hospital with these same symptoms.

She continued to have everything. I always felt if there was an illness out there, that one out of every two people would get, she got it. I was safe. Even after I found out I was diabetic, I did not have any dramatic changes to my health. In fact, I still felt good. So, I did not listen to my doctors and did not take care of myself.

I did, however, think this was so strange. I had been diagnosed, but Merry had not. I asked her about her blood sugar. She said that she was not diabetic, as if it were something to be ashamed of. In fact, she was hypoglycemic. Knowing a little about diabetes, I told her she needed to watch her blood sugar. She laughed, even when I told her I thought our mother had been diabetic. I was the little sister and was not as wise as she.

A few months later, Merry told me the rose scratches on her arms were not healing and I insisted she get to the doctor immediately to have her blood sugar checked. She did and found that she had become diabetic. She even agreed that mother was probably diabetic, too.

Her diabetes progressed more rapidly than mine, resulting in strokes, taking her mind a little at a time. During the summer, she had some short-term memory loss but was able to officiate at her granddaughter's wedding.

She was beautiful. Her eyes glowed; her hair sparkled, even her skin was clear.

We laughed and shared stories of our youth. Neither of us remembered things quite the same way. But we did remember how much we loved one another.

Over the next few months, I would call her and leave messages on her phone. But she failed to call me back. Christmas Eve I went to see her. The glow was gone. She was gone. Christmas day she fell into a coma and stopped breathing two days later.

We never found out what her original illness was. I think it was some auto-immune deficiency, but I will never know. I just hope she will forgive me for my callousness. I cannot rely on her to be the one to get sick now; I guess I will have to take better care of myself. I should have started earlier. I just wish we could have been old women together.

WAGON TRAINS ON A HIGHWAY
Jan Zimmerman

A white line on a oasis of black,

shapes of sunset cunning as wood, metal and a canvas moving,

animals straining as children guide them

through the early morning fog.

Slivers of sunlight

slowly peeping through misty shadows,

cigarettes shared in the darkness of half-dawn….

Words shared and memories traded

another day has started.

Twenty miles to go

and sixty-three children who need love and trust,

One road behind us

a thousand miles to go.

I look at the faces of youth who should be our tomorrow

and I wonder if their die is cast,

Will the world audit in their favor?

The fog is lifting, time to move out….

winding roads and a lot of time

can we help to erase the hate and pain?

TEACHER IN DISTRESS
Mary Barton

"Word is that it was pretty bad out there in the grazing field today," said the secretary as I passed through the main office walking toward my own office.

It was Friday afternoon at the end of a very hectic week. Several years of experience working with junior high age kids had convinced me that those years were the most important, most challenging, most exciting, and most dangerous years to which a teacher could choose to dedicate his or her career. In fact, I felt that connecting with these kids held some of our greatest hopes for shaping and molding the future of our society. It was still early in my administrative career and some days—especially days like that one—made me wonder if I had been deluding myself when I had made that choice.

"Yes, the kids were pretty unruly. Even a little bit of food throwing went on, but that often happens on Friday afternoons." I hesitated, then added, "I'm tired already, but I have a lot of paperwork to finish before I can go home today. I'm closing my door; please do not let anyone in except cases which you consider to be dire emergencies. Thanks for helping, Anita," I said as I went into my office and closed the door behind me.

Unfortunately, I was not to have a peaceful minute that afternoon.

I had just sat down and pulled out my paperwork when Anita was at the door calling my name. "I'm sorry to bother you, Mrs. Carruth," she said as she knocked on the door then opened it. "I think this is one of those emergencies you mentioned. One of the students just came with a note from Mr. Benjamin asking that you come down to room B12 immediately. According to the student, there is a problem with one of the teachers."

Knowing that B12 was Miss Taylor's room and also knowing that Edith Taylor was often unpredictable, I hurried out of the office and down to the room. Edith was a single, fiftyish woman who was most anxious to be accepted by the younger teachers with whom she worked. She had shoulder length gray hair turned under pageboy fashion. Long squared off bangs fell across her forehead, and her eyes were a steely gray to match.

As I opened the door, Mr. Benjamin signaled me to wait outside, and he came to join me. When he closed the door, I heard the students in the room giggling and becoming more and more unruly.

"We had better make this quick," Ed Benjamin said. "Those kids are higher than kites. I told Edith to go over to the teachers' lounge and I would take care of her class until someone else is able to do it. This is my prep period, but I have a class after that, so someone will need to cover the last period of the day." He glanced down the hall. "Now you better hurry over to the lounge, because Edith was pretty upset when she left here. I'll stop by your office after school to fill you in on anything you still don't know."

Thanking Ed, I hurried over to the teachers' lounge. As I entered the coffee room, the front part of the teachers' lounge, the teachers there asked if I was looking for Edith. "Why yes, I am. Do you know where she is?" I asked.

The teachers there all nodded toward the back room which is called the cot room.

"Thanks," I said and walked to the other room.

As I entered the darkened room, I saw her lying on one of the cots. "Are you okay, Edith?" I asked.

Edith sat up on the side of the cot and began sobbing. "I'm so embarrassed! I can never face those kids again! I guess it's my fault, but kids today are little terrors. I really hate teaching those brats."

"Now Edith," I said gently. "Relax while I get you a cold drink. Would you rather have water or a bottle of pop?"

"Water is okay," she responded, "but I don't even know if I can get it down."

After getting a bottle of water from the small refrigerator which was located just outside the door in the coffee room, I handed it to Edith. I sat down on a chair beside the cot. "Take your time," I said. "When you are ready, please tell me what happened in your classroom today."

"Oh, it was simply awful," Edith said on a sob. "You know, in my classroom I'm strict, but I'm fair. Not only do I insist the students follow

117

the rules, but I follow them myself. One thing I cannot abide is the students passing notes to each other during class time. I have a very strict rule about that. When a student is caught passing a note, he or she has to come up in front of the classroom and read the note to the whole class."

She took a second to compose herself. "Right after we got back from lunch today, one of the boys in the back walked up to the trash can. On the way, he put a note on the desk of one of the girls he passed. The girl had not opened it. So, I told him he had to come to the front of the room and read it." She bristled. "He had the nerve to tell me that he could not and would not read it out loud."

Stiffening even more, she said, "When I told him that he either read the note or I would send him to the vice principal's office, he told me he didn't think I would want to hear the note. I assured him that if there was no foul language in it, he could sit down after reading it and that would be the end of the matter. He asked if he would be sent to the office if I didn't like it. I told him again that if he had not used profanity, I would let it go by this time."

She blew out a breath. "I could tell the note was very short, and I assumed it would not be too bad. I told the boy—Pete is his name—to go ahead and read it and quit wasting time. Pretending to look at the note, but looking beyond it to the other students, he said, 'Did you know Miss. Taylor is a queer?'"

At that time Edith began to sob again. She covered her face with her hands and curled up on the cot with her back to me. She shook all over, and I was afraid she would be sick. "It's okay to cry, Edith, worse things have happened around here. We can work this out," I added.

"No," said Edith. "Those kids will never forget that scene.

"You're right. They won't forget that silly scene you and they played out," I said calmly. "But, with some thought and planning, you and I can turn this into a learning situation for all of you."

When she looked at me, I said, "You will need to admit that you could have handled some things better. Together we will stress the importance of young people treating others with respect. You might also think about telling them, or showing them, in some way, that you respect them, too."

Trying to stay patient, I said, "Now, Edith, I want you to go into the bathroom and wash your face. While you're doing that, I will go to your classroom and get your purse. After you pick up your purse from me in the office, you will go home and relax. Do something you enjoy doing. Try not to ruminate on what has happened here this afternoon."

I hoped I was doing the right thing. "First thing on Monday morning you and I will meet in the office. We'll plan exactly what will happen as you go to each of your classes during the day. Are you okay with that, Edith?"

"No, not really, but I don't know what else to do. I can't afford to quit my job," Edith said between sobs. "If you will help me, maybe I can do it."

"Well, lets you and I take this one step at a time," I said as I left to go to her classroom for her purse.

When I arrived there, I realized I needed to say something to the students. After asking the substitute teacher for a minute to speak to the class, I cleared my throat and began improvising as I went. "You know, boys and girls, when I tell people about the school where I work, I tell them how proud I am of the behavior of the students who attend here. Generally speaking, you are all well mannered, cooperative, well behaved young people."

I gave them my most serious look. "Today, however; at least some of you in this room behaved very badly. I don't believe in punishing the whole group for the behavior of two or three. I know that one young man was very much out of line. But I think it's likely that inappropriate comments were made by several of you, perhaps even before and after the act.

"Pete, I want you to accompany me when I leave this room. We will deal with your problem in my office." I glanced around the room. "As for the rest of you, I plan to continue my conversation here with you next week. Let's hope we can all learn from what happened here today."

As I walked back to my office, I thought about the situation. I was weary and still had a lot to do before going home. I knew it would be a very difficult weekend for Edith, and I hated having to take her problem home with me. I knew, however, that it was extremely important for her to be able to regain a reasonable relationship with the students she would necessarily continue to teach.

When we reached the main office, I told Pete to wait on the bench outside my office while I talked with Ms. Taylor. When Edith arrived,

I met her and walked into my office with her, more than anything to prevent Pete from making comments as she passed him. As we moved inside, I invited her to sit down while I closed the door.

"I know I told you to go home and relax, Edith, but I know it will be hard to avoid thinking about next week. You will replay many times the embarrassing minutes which caused your distress. With that in mind, I'm going to give you some points I would like for you to think about."

She watched me anxiously.

"You might create a plan for setting things straight when you come back on Monday. Think about what you will say to your fifth hour class. Probably you will want to say something to those children in your other classes, too.

"I would like to give you some points to consider as you outline how you intend to reintegrate with your kids. Is that okay so far? I know you're really shaken now, but together we can get through this. Probably the sooner you outline in your mind how you intend to begin the week on Monday, the better you will feel and the more you will be able to relax. Most of all, I care about you. I want to help you get through this in a way that will allow you to feel comfortable in your job, okay?"

Edith sobbed and rubbed her red eyes and tear streaked face with a wadded tissue, but she nodded so I continued.

"First. What good things can you tell your students about how well you like teaching them? They will be apprehensive about what you're going to say. I'm sure they're expecting you to yell at them about what happened today.

"Second. I would like for you to say something about your rules and the importance of having them. You can emphasize how much you try to be fair, and the fact that you try to follow the rules the same as you expect them to. You can also tell them you believe sometimes rules need to be changed, and that you're thinking this is a time to review your own rules."

Seeing that Edith was cautiously listening, I went on. "Next you can tell them how badly you felt today. Emphasize that you're talking about your own personal embarrassment. You might add that you like our school because our students are usually quite thoughtful. Not only do you observe politeness and concern expressed by them for each other, but also for our staff.

"Lastly, tell them that you have begun revising your classroom rules to avoid circumstances like what happened today. If you think you can manage the situation, you might ask if they have suggestions that might be helpful. Be sure not to let it get out of hand with silliness. Tell them that you will review the new rules with me so we can agree on the appropriateness of them for your particular classes."

I smiled kindly at her. "I hope that will help you plan for your return. It is up to you, but if you wish, I will plan to be in your fifth period class as it convenes on Monday. I truly believe that if we handle this the right way your classes will go smoothly that day and, hopefully, on the days that follow. What do you think, Edith?"

"Okay," she answered as if her thoughts were a long way away.

"Do you think you feel well enough to drive?" I asked.

Edith nodded as she choked out another sob and wiped her eyes with a tissue from the box I always kept on the corner of my desk.

"If you wish, you can sit there until you gain a little more composure. Feel free to leave when you are ready."

I glanced toward the closed door. "Now, I'm going to talk to Pete and take him down to the Boys Vice Principal's office." I left her and went out into the main office where he was sitting alone on the bench.

"Pete, I do not approve of your behavior in the classroom today. I expect better than that from all our students. You must respect our teachers, if you want them to respect you as a person. Now, let's go down the hall to Mr. Brown's office."

When I returned to my office it was 2:45 and school was out at 3 o'clock. That left just about enough time for me to get out in front of the school to supervise the students who were boarding the buses. Paperwork would have to wait. My workday had begun at 7:30 that morning and it would be 3:45 before I could get back to my office. Two hours for necessary paperwork should allow me to be on my way home by 6:00.

"I love my job, but I love the weekends."

LIFE'S TWISTS AND TURNS
Starla Criser

She was at it again.

Jared froze, coffee cup in hand, in the doorway to the patio. His new neighbor wearing body hugging leotard and tights was gracefully bending forward, eyes closed. She leaned over until her palms flattened on the rug covering her adjoining patio. He should probably go back inside his apartment and give her some privacy.

Yet he found himself rooted to the spot. He watched, mesmerized, as she slowly lifted her legs, bending them, moving until her knees rested on her elbows. He gaped in amazement. How could she do that? With his bad back, he had trouble bending to reach his knees.

His pulse had stepped up a good twenty beats, probably more. He told himself it wasn't because he admired her slender, well-toned form. Heavens, he was a sixty-eight-year-old man. His days of… Well, they were long over with. No, his reaction was simply because of the shocking things she could do with her body.

"Good morning, Jared," Ann Marie Tyler said casually, saving him from his crazy thoughts. She turned her head to look his way. Her chin-length, white hair swaying with the movement nearly brushed the rug. She had to be somewhere around the upper sixties, like him. But she sure didn't look it.

"Uh…good morning," he said nervously, tightening his hold on his cup and stepped outside.

She smiled, the faint lines around her mouth deepening. Her gaze seemed to sweep slowly over him from his sock-covered feet to his Bermuda shorts to his loose-fitting T-shirt. Self-conscious, he sucked in his gut and pushed his shoulders back. He hadn't thought about how far he was out of condition, until she studied him. Maybe he needed to spend a little time at the gym.

Deciding he didn't want to think too hard along that line, he asked, "You do this every morning?" Stupid question. He'd already seen her doing this nearly every morning since she'd moved into the active senior apartment complex almost a month ago.

An early riser, he'd been comfortable with stepping out onto his patio just after dawn to enjoy his first cup of coffee, especially now that it was spring. He'd sit in his cushioned rocker, sip the hot brew, and listen to the birds in the nearby trees. Retired and widowed, he had plenty of time for observing nature. Plenty of time for contemplating what he might or might not do that day.

But Ann Marie had messed up those peaceful times. His old heart couldn't keep starting his days spotting his neighbor in one eye-catching outfit after another, contorting her body in some bizarre way. She was going to drive him to an early grave.

"A little yoga first thing in the morning gets me ready for whatever comes along that day," she said, closing her eyes again.

She appeared at ease in that strange position. How could that be? Even just observing her, his arms empathized with hers, felt strained from tightened muscles.

Quietly watching her, he considered the other quirky things he'd discovered about the woman. With the nice weather, he often had his patio door open to let in a fresh breeze through the screen door. Her door was usually open, too. Many times, he'd heard her singing along to show tunes from the past, slightly off-key. It always made him smile. His beloved wife had also not been blessed with musical ability. It had made her self-conscious and she'd rarely sang, not even in church. But Ann Marie wasn't bothered by her lack of talent. She sang her heart out. In fact, she was humming now, which made him smile.

She seemed to enjoy all kinds of music. Often her radio played everything from the oldies-but-goodies, to Elvis Presley, to Fats Domino, to Country Western, even to that crazy hip-hop stuff and rap. Usually it was pretty loud, too. But he'd never complained, more amused than annoyed.

He knew she danced in her apartment as well. He'd been standing out on his patio, by the railing, looking around, when he'd glanced into her place by accident. The music had been turned up, of course. She'd been twisting, and grinning in pure happiness. A dance he'd never mastered.

He was a terrible dancer, something his wife had teased him about.

Ann Marie began moving again, capturing his attention. Her feet flattened on the rug once more, and then she began walking her hands back, slowly slid them up her lithe body until she was standing. "There," she said, sounding satisfied. "I feel so much better."

"Right. Better," he responded doubtfully. He expected to see her arms trembling after holding her weight for so long, expected to see weariness on her face. Instead, she looked energized, like that bunny in the ads.

Her pretty blue eyes sparkled and she zeroed in on his coffee cup. "Yoga is far better for you than a jolt of coffee, trust me."

"But I like that jolt. I like coffee," he grumbled. Okay, his doctor had told him to cut back on the amount he drank daily. His compromise had been to invest in a Keurig coffeemaker that brewed one cup at a time, instead of having a whole pot available all day long.

"Green tea would be healthier."

He'd always considered that it would be like drinking pond water. No thanks. He took another sip of coffee that had already started cooling, deciding to withhold his opinion. He didn't want to argue with her.

She reached for a hand towel on the arm of a wicker chair next to her. Lightly wiping at the faint sheen of sweat on her brow, she studied him, as if waiting for an answer.

"I'm healthy enough." He'd gone back to holding in his gut, but doubted he was fooling her. It wasn't that he had a bulging beer belly or anything. Still...

She flashed him a tolerant smile. He noticed a slight gap in her front teeth. It was endearing and he liked discovering that she wasn't as near-perfect as he'd first thought.

"Have you ever tried yoga?"

"I exercise." The words "liar, liar, pants on fire" passed through his thoughts.

One of her thin eyebrows lifted. "Really? Do you belong to the Y or an exercise club?"

When his beloved Sarah had been alive, she'd tried to get him to go with her to the YMCA. She'd gone on and on about the abundance of exercise equipment, about the pool for swimming laps, and about the many kinds of classes. But he'd never managed to go. He'd told her he got plenty of exercise walking around in the classroom as he taught high school shop classes. Plus, he helped with coaching boys' basketball. And there was the huge lawn he used to mow when they still had a house in the suburbs. He didn't have any of that these days.

"I walk around the park several times a week," he stated defensively, feeling guilty at the same time. Okay, his outings had faded back to maybe twice a week, sometimes once a week.

"Good for you," she said, dropping the towel. She raised her arms to shoulder level and began doing side-to-side twists. "At least that's something."

He watched, not the least bit tempted to do it himself. Her arms were slender, with barely a hint of the droopy wings many women complained about having as they aged. Not that he'd really noticed, except when his wife had moaned about it. And he'd tried to tell he it wasn't any big deal. He'd been better off keeping his mouth shut.

"Occasionally I play golf," he added, although he couldn't remember the last time he had.

"My husband used to play regularly." She did some more twisting, smiling thoughtfully. "He never could convince me to go with him. I didn't see much sense in hitting a small ball around like that." She stopped for a second. "I used to play tennis."

He'd figured that she was a widow, but he never knew quite what to say about that. So, he simply said, "I've never played tennis." He thought about something he'd read in the last senior center newsletter. "It seems people are playing pickleball now. Maybe I should try that."

"I've heard about it, too. Sounds interesting." She went back to twisting around. Her hair brushed back and forth across her cheeks. He noticed a faint white scar on the side of her neck, wondered how she'd gotten it. But he wouldn't ask, too personal.

"Well, I think it's time I went back inside." He gave her a look of challenge and held up his cup. "Coffee has grown cold. Time to fix a new cup."

She chuckled, her eyes dancing in amusement. "Green tea would be better."

"Not happening." He turned to go back into his apartment, realizing he'd enjoyed their first real conversation. Maybe you could become friends, just friends. He didn't have any lady friends, hadn't even thought about it before. But maybe you should.

"You should come try the yoga class I teach at the senior center."

Her invitation caught him off-guard. He immediately had visions of watching her contorting in all kinds of bizarre poses. Then he saw himself trying them and failing miserably. Too tough on a man's ego.

"Thanks, but I'll stick to walking in the park." Safer. Less potentially embarrassing, too.

"If you change your mind," she said softly, "you're always welcome."

***

Ann Marie had just spread another large blue cushioned mat on the floor of the main exercise room when she heard footsteps in the doorway. Her regulars were arriving. She was always happy to see them, glad to visit with the dozen older women who came to her classes. A couple were already becoming good friends.

She listened to the sound of them putting their purses and water bottles on the table along the wall. Several of them started conversations, one laughed at something someone had said. All of it made her smile as she turned to face her students.

But it was the uncomfortable-looking man in black exercise shorts that hung to his knees and a loose-fitting black T-shirt that snagged her attention. She blinked in surprise. Jared Baker. It had been over a week since she'd talked to him on their adjoining patios. Not for a second had she seriously thought he would come to her class.

The other women were sizing him up, trying not to flat-out stare at him. Only rarely did a man join their class of active seniors. The men who came to this center seemed to shy away from the mostly-female classes. They mainly played pool or cards or hung out in the TV room. So, she knew how much guts it had taken for Jared to come today…and to not turn around and run for his life.

She hurried toward him, smiling. "Decided to try it, did you? I'm so glad."

He appeared relieved that she'd come to his rescue. The tightness in his jaw eased; his brown eyes didn't look so worried. "I actually came to try out pickleball, but it doesn't start for another hour. So…"

He hadn't come in response to her invitation. She felt slightly disappointed. Still, she had him here and that was a huge step. Others in their apartment complex had commented a time or two that he was a nice man. They thought he was lonely, but he tended to keep to himself. And, yes, she'd also learned that quite a few of the widowed women had tried to entice him to join in their occasional social events. Some had even taken him casseroles or special desserts that might draw him out. It hadn't worked. She imagined that her dear husband would have reacted much the same way. Which made her realize that she had a soft spot in her heart for him.

Boldly, she stepped closer and took hold of his hand. He stiffened but didn't jerk free, which pleased her. Ignoring the questioning looks they were getting, she tugged him with her toward the nearest mat, safely at the back of the room.

When she stopped and released him, she gave him a teasing smile. "Bet you thought I was going to lead you to one of the mats up front."

"Yep, I was afraid of that." A hint of a smile lifted one corner of his mouth. "This will be much better…for both of us."

She liked the sound of his deep voice, the slight rumble to it. She also liked his neatly-trimmed band of white hair and his short beard. Her husband had gone completely bald early in their marriage, but she'd never minded. Unlike Tom, who had been about her same height, Jared stood a good six inches taller than her. His shoulders were broad; his arms still fairly toned. But he did have a slight paunch. Inwardly she smiled at remembering how he'd tried to hide it from her.

Her gaze shifted to the wall clock and she made her way to the front of the room. The women had found their favorite spots, ready for the class to begin. Although she caught a few of them glancing back toward the strange man in their midst. While she had loved her husband for over forty years and was still adjusting to his loss, she couldn't deny that her new neighbor intrigued her. She cherished her close friends and spending time with them. But she missed having a man around to talk with, to disagree with, to challenge. She didn't want anything more than that.

She looked across the room, found Jared watching her. Their gazes met for just a second. Something connected between them, something she couldn't explain. But it filled her with peace.

Flashing him a challenging look, she said, "Let's take it to the mat, ladies…and gentleman. We'll start with the lotus pose."

As she sat down, knees out wide, she drew her heels close. Her students followed her demonstration as best they could. Even Jared made a valiant attempt, with a quiet groan. Still, he tried.

"Have I mentioned lately, everyone, how good for the body green tea is?" She couldn't resist looking at Jared again. Her lips twitched at the roll of his eyes. "Some say it tastes like…"

"Pond scum," he volunteered. His face reddened when the ladies glanced at him, a couple giggling.

She, too, laughed. "Perhaps we can have a private discussion on the matter sometime."

"Perhaps," he muttered, then focused on attempting to pull his heels close to his body, grimacing from the effort.

Ah, a baby step. She found herself eager to finish the class, eager to get home. She might just make him a big glass of green tea and get him to sit with her on their patios. They could talk about… Well, anything.

YOU WEAR IT WELL!
Cherise Langenberg

If you have lived 100 years—
you have lived to see....

36,500 sunrises and sunsets,
1,300 full moons,
25 leap years,
3.5 years of waiting at red lights,
9 months of opening up junk mail.

You have lived through 24 Presidents,
and numerous years of election campaigns.

You have lived through changes in planes, trains, and automobiles.

You have lived through "numerous" new inventions,
and the return of old ones!

You have made it through the Kansas storms—
tornadoes and all!

You have lived to see years of family,
children, grandchildren, great-grandchildren
and the great-greats!

You have seen many years of
smiles, laughter, tears and miracles of joy.

You have had 2,555,000 hours of sleep,
numerous years of working, and numerous years of resting.

You have "RE-FIRED"—NOT retired!

YOU HAVE WISDOM THROUGH THE AGES—
AND YOU WEAR IT WELL!
CONGRATULATIONS!

A CAR JUST DROVE IN MY CLASSROOM
Mary Barton

Lunch supervision was over, kids and teachers were back in their classrooms, and the campus seemed to be quiet. Great, I thought as I entered my office and closed the door. Hopefully, I would be able to complete paperwork which had been waiting for me for a couple of days.

As I sat down behind my desk and pulled out the paperwork from my top drawer, the lights in my office winked and then went out. Because of the shade and bushes outside my windows, there was not enough light anytime of the day for me to do paperwork without the lights being on.

Rising from my chair, I walked to the door and opened it. I intended to ask my secretary, Anita, if she had any idea why we had lost electric power. It was obvious, however; the lights in the outer office and in the darkened hallway were all out.

As I walked towards the outer door, Anita commented, "I would say all the lights in the building are out. Hopefully, the rest of the campus is okay, but I'll bet it isn't."

"From the noise that's generating outside, I would venture to say we have a big problem. I'm on my way to see how much damage there is. Wish me luck; this could be a very long afternoon," I said as I hurried out into the corridor.

"If Duane comes back in here—I think he's in the lounge, tell him I'm starting out on the east side of the campus in I Building. I'll leave the west side and the gym to him." I was sure, Duane, our principal, would finish smoking a cigarette before returning to the office. He said regularly that after lunch supervision he had earned that privilege.

As I passed through the corridor to the end of the hall, I saw at least one person standing in the doorway of each classroom in A Building. All of them looked confused. So, I was able to quickly deduct that all the lights were out in that building. I stopped in at each room and told the teacher to keep their students inside their rooms. Since the regular passing time would not be for at least 45 minutes, we would have to ring a bell to signal when to release their students.

Walking through the cafeteria and the outdoor lunch pavilion, I headed toward I Building, which ran along the most easterly border of the school campus.

As I entered the door at one end of the building, I found the hallway alive and churning with students and their teachers. Everyone was yelling. To get control of the chaos, teachers struggled to talk over the noise that the kids made.

One of the teachers hurried up to me and said, "Mr. Hoyt yelled for us all to get out of the building before it explodes."

"Did Mr. Hoyt say why he thought the building was going to explode?" I asked, as I helped get everyone out through one of the two doors, one at each end, leading outside.

"He said something about a car in his room," said the same teacher. "It didn't make sense to me. If there was an emergency, I thought it best to get the kids out and then ask why."

"That was good thinking I would say, Doris," I said, as I hurried the remaining people out of the building.

Looking around for Mr. Hoyt, I saw him running at the head of the pack at the far side of the athletic field. Heading in that direction, I motioned to Henry Hoyt to meet me part way over to where I was. It was a very large athletic field and I had on medium-heel pumps.

Hesitatingly, he began walking toward me, shouting something that I could not understand.

As we neared a point near the middle of the field, I yelled to him asking if he were the one responsible for the evacuation of I Building.

"Actually, it was the kids," he answered breathlessly. "I was so scared, I ran."

"What were you scared of?" I asked.

"Didn't you see it?" he yelled. "Didn't you see that car in my room?"

"Henry, when I came by your room, the doors were closed. So, no, I didn't see a car in your room. Now slow down and let me get this straight. Somehow a car came into your room, and you ran. Am I right so far?"

"Yes, Lucy, that's what I'm trying to tell you," said Henry Hoyt. "A Chevy drove through the wall and knocked the typewriters on the floor," he said, stammering so hard it was difficult to understand him.

"If you don't mind, Henry, would you please explain to me how the car got into your room?" I asked.

"Well, I was standing at the door as we are supposed to during passing. I didn't really see it happen, but I heard it. It was a huge crash. The typewriters went flying. Luckily there weren't any students at the typewriters on the ledge by the window."

"So, Henry, I'm assuming someone was driving the car down the alley behind the building. Am I right so far?"

"Yes, according to the kids who were watching out the window, there were two cars racing down the alley. Now you know that alley gets narrow right there by the end of the building. I guess that's because of all the electric and other utility poles there. Well, the guy in the Chevy must've been going pretty fast. I assume he turned out to try to avoid hitting the poles. One of the poles was broken off at a level about the height of the car. And the front end of that Chevy was sticking right into the wall where two typewriters had been a minute before."

"I assume you told the children to line up, and you headed out the door at the end of the building."

"Well," Henry said, "I surveyed the situation and decided it was best to vacate the room.

"I knew we had a dangerous situation there. What if there were power lines down and there was gas coming out of that car? What if those lines got into the gas and sparked a fire?

"I figured that whole end of the building might blow up any minute, so I ran! I couldn't think what to say, and I knew if I ran out the kids would follow me. I was right, they ran right out of the building after me." As he described his situation to me, he began to shake uncontrollably.

"Well, I guess you're right. The most important thing was to get the children out. I am glad you did that," I said with a more positive tone than I really felt.

I wish I could report that you made sure all the kids got out safely. It would also be encouraging to hear you report that you had methodically sent a couple of students to notify other teachers and children in I Building.

"Line your kids up out here by the fence. Have them sit down on the ground," I said. "Keep them in that area. We don't want people roaming all over the campus. We have no intercom and no way to get the attention of all 1500 kids in these buildings."

With Mr. Hoyt's class in place, I approached the other teachers of classes which had evacuated I Building and instructed them to have their children sit down where they were standing. "Please keep them there until you receive further instructions. Do not let your students go back to any of the buildings. Keep them here at the far side of the athletic field. We will keep the other students in their classrooms inside the other buildings."

With that, I headed back to the alley on the far side of I Building to see what I could, without going in the building. I wanted to know just what had happened to cause us to have this schoolwide problem. When I got there, I saw that, in truth, there was a '57 Chevrolet with about half of the front end sticking through the wall and into the class where the typewriters were. Moving on up to where the car was, I saw that there were power lines hanging down. None touched the ground or the car. It did not appear that we were in danger of an explosion.

By that time, the crowd of people from the businesses which were located on the other side of the alley began to gather around where the accident had taken place. Soon the fire department, the electric company, the telephone company, the police, and many other emergency vehicles had arranged themselves around the wrecked car.

Obviously, we were not in danger of fire or explosion, but we were without power. That would interrupt school activities for the last two hours of the day. Heading back to the administration building, I found the principal, Duane, coming toward me with a "what are we going to do now?" look on his face.

"According to the emergency people, it will be hours before they can get this situation taken care of," I said. "It seems to me, that it will be necessary for us to keep the kids in the classrooms where they are now until time for them to go home at 3 o'clock," I added when the two of us were close enough to discuss the situation. "They will be a handful for their teachers. But we would have chaos if we let them out of their rooms at the end of this class period."

"I think you are right, Lucy," Duane said. "Let's put the classes from I Building over in the auditorium. We can let them go back—one class at a time—to get their things from the classrooms in that building. I think that would be easier than to have the teachers try to manage them there where all the action is."

"I agree," I said. "I'll start over here with these kids that are on the field, and give them and their teachers instructions. After that I'll go to the administration building and B Building to give those teachers instructions for keeping the kids in place until the end of the school day."

"It won't be easy for any of us," he said, "I'll go to H Building and the gym classes to give them instructions."

"You're right," I said, "but most of our teachers have enough experience to know that to keep the lid on, we will have to be inventive. I guess you could say we are all working outside the box."

"Okay, Lucy, let's go see if we can put lids on all the hotspots. When it looks like everyone is doing okay—and all is calm, you and I can meet at the middle doors of the administration building. We will need to discuss plans for getting the children off campus at the end of the day, without having everyone trying to see what's going on in the alley."

"Sounds like a plan to me," I said. "I'm on my way. I'll see you in about 15 minutes. If we locate ourselves in that area, we can be seen by most of the teachers on the campus. Hopefully, our vigilance will prevent them from getting too stressed out."

"One more thing," Duane said. "Let's tell the teachers to dismiss students who ride school buses at 2:45. And then dismiss the others to go home at 3 o'clock?"

"That's a good idea," I said. "Also, the teachers should warn their students not to go near the alley. I suspect the emergency vehicles will still have that area barricaded anyway. Let's ask teachers and staff who don't have students that last hour to help us spread out across the north end of the campus and direct the students around the other way."

Each of us went in opposite directions, and soon there was a relative calm throughout the large campus. Surprisingly, the rest of the afternoon went smoothly. Needless to say, the whole staff was pretty much exhausted by the time all the kids had left the campus.

***

"Hey, Duane," I said, as we walked to the parking lot after work that day, "I think you need to talk to Henry about the manner in which he provided for the safety of his class. Ha ha."

"You're right, but I think I would like you to be in on that. Do you have time right now that we could go get a cup of coffee and discuss the approach we will take with him tomorrow?"

"Yes, I'll make time. I think it's important that we take care of it right away. Let's meet at the Cup and Saucer over on the Boulevard."

We each got into our own cars and headed towards our favorite coffee shop.

"This will not be easy," Duane said, with a frown, as we sat down in a booth in the back of the Cup and Saucer's dining room. "He does not take criticism well."

"I've noticed that," I said. "Sometimes I get the feeling he expects Bob and me to take care of all his discipline problems. So he can play the part of the good guy."

"I know, it won't be easy. It may seem like we're wasting our breath, but I do feel it has to be done," he said.

For more than an hour we drank coffee and talked about each of the mistakes in judgment we had seen Henry display. When we agreed we had included everything, we shook our heads and sighed.

"You know, Duane, we are setting ourselves up for an impossible task. If he hears the first item, I'll be surprised. As soon as it's out of your mouth, he will insist on telling his side of the story. I have never once heard him accept responsibility for anything."

"You're right. But we can't let this go by without putting it in his record. You know the rules about that. He must be allowed to defend his position on anything that goes into his record."

"It might work better if you asked him to tell you how he feels about the situation," I said.

"And we will, too," he said. "First, Lucy, we are in this together—you and me. Second, I suspect he will insist on talking about everyone else's mistakes, but not any of his own. He is pretty good at giving advice, especially after the fact."

"Yes, I'm afraid you are right, but we must start someplace," I said. "Let's sit down with him and begin with asking him to describe what happened. If he insists on placing blame, we can start with items at the top of our list."

"Okay. Let's see if you and I can agree on the top five items on our list, then call it quits for this afternoon. I will arrange for a substitute teacher for his first period class. We will meet with him in my office the first thing in the morning."

Duane paid for our coffee and we both left, knowing that each of us would think of little else until the next morning.

***

Apparently, Henry had the same problem. The following morning a substitute teacher reported to teach his classes. Since teachers needing to be absent from school were responsible for calling a service at the district office to request a substitute be sent to fill in his or her assignment, it was not unusual for a sub to show up before we heard from the teacher.

Customarily, however; the teacher needing to be absent also called an administrator in the school in which he or she worked. When it came time for school to begin, and we had not heard from Henry, it became my job to contact him for details of his absence.

After several rings, Henry's wife answered the phone. She reported that Henry was too sick to talk on the phone. When I asked her if he had lesson plans prepared, she said she would have him call me as soon as he was able.

It seemed, however, that he continued to get worse. At the end of the day, Mrs. Hoyt called to say she had made an appointment with the doctor for Henry for the next day. And we should retain the sub for another day.

In the afternoon of the following day, Mrs. Hoyt called to say Henry had some bug and would be out until the end of the week. At that time, I reminded her that would be more than three days, and he would need a report from the doctor when he returned.

On the next Monday, I got another call from Mrs. Hoyt. She said that the doctor had ordered Henry in for more tests, and he would be out for several more days.

✶✶✶

After eight days of absence, Henry returned to work with a report from a Dr. Woodward stating that he was under his care for treatment of ulcers. The day he finally returned Duane was away at a district wide meeting. When he returned, other responsibilities prevented us from being able to schedule a time when we could meet with Henry.

The following week was spring vacation. When we all returned to school, the meeting with Henry was postponed several times, because the right time never seemed to be available.

Miraculously, Henry's health seemed to improve; perhaps that was because he had used up all his sick days.

✶✶✶

Later that spring, he dropped into my office one afternoon. He said,

"Lucy, I have a favor to ask of you. I am completing work toward my administrative credential this spring. I wonder if you would complete this recommendation form for my placement file."

Needless to say, I was overwhelmed that this man would consider himself to be leadership material. He hoped to be assigned to a school where he would be responsible for the programs and safety of many students and adults. I was, in fact, speechless.

Finally, I said, "Sit down, Henry. I need to think about this. You realize, if I were to do this, I would be telling others that I think you would make a good administrator."

"Well," Henry said, "that is what I hope you will do."

"And what would you say I should base this recommendation on?"

"I assume you are my friend. You are always pleasant to me when I see you and when you come to my classroom. You have never said anything that would make me think anything else," he said with a confused look on his face.

"I think, Henry, that I have left some things unsaid. For instance, could you see me or either of the other two administrators behaving the way you did on the day of the wreck? If you want to leave your form here you may, but I'm pretty sure I can't complete it in the way you would like for me to."

With that, Henry picked up his packet and said as he was leaving, "Maybe you're not such a good administrator after all."

I would like to have said, "Back at you, Henry." But I didn't.

MR. LEBOWITZ'S CHOIR
Mary Barton

"Good morning, Lucy. I wonder if I might have a few minutes of your time?" asked Mr. Leibowitz before school one Monday morning in early September.

"Certainly, Aaron, have a seat. We can close the door if you like," I answered, motioning toward the choral music teacher, who stood in the door of my small office. "How can I help you?" I sat back in my own chair.

"This is a very big request," he said. "I need to start by telling you about last year, which was my first year here at Eastland. As you probably know, my assignment is to teach choral music classes, and do some coaching after school. First let me say, I really love these assignments. I work hard to do well in both areas. Perhaps you don't know—or maybe you do—choral music is not currently considered to be an important part of any student's education. I—for one—consider both music and sports very important in educating the children in school today."

He drew in a breath. "That is the first reason why I am making this large request. The second reason is I am hoping that the students here can make a big splash in the music competitions in Los Angeles County next spring. In fact, I would be ecstatic if our kids could prove to be good enough to go to the state level."

"Now, I know," he continued, "that Eastland is considered to be the most disadvantaged junior high school in the district. You and I understand that the cause is—in general—discrimination within the community against our brown-skinned, dark-eyed pupils. With enough creativity, I believe we can change our position in the scheme of things here in Los Angeles County. And, hopefully, in years to come we will hold a recognizable position in all of Southern California."

'Well, Aaron, I really do appreciate your enthusiasm. How do you propose we gain this magnificent status for Eastland?" I asked.

"You may not believe this, but we ended last year with a combined mixed choir of just over 200 students. This year my plan is to make that 400. Now, I'm sure you are aware that there is no such class listed on the schedule for this year. I have been running this group as an afterschool activity two nights a week. Believe it or not, the kids are staying," he said proudly.

"You're right, I can't believe you've gotten that many kids to stay after school on a regular basis for a music program. I know they will stay and work hard to be in the sports program, but I certainly have never seen it in a music program. Please tell me more," I said, excited and interested.

"As is stipulated in my teaching assignment, I coach the younger boys in football and basketball. When I began recruiting for those teams, I let it be known that guys in my music classes would have a better chance of getting on athletic teams, if they were actively involved in the music program.

"When they came to try out for the teams, I asked each boy if he would be willing to participate in the music program. As you know, all seventh graders are enrolled in a music class. Eighth and ninth graders can take choir as an elective. If they showed interest, I told the boys who were not currently enrolled in a music class that I could probably get their schedules changed. I even told them that their nonathletic friends might be able to get the same deal if they could sing. Since I teach nearly all the music classes—except instrumental music—I didn't figure that would be a big problem. It seems I got away with it, and we won some ballgames, too," Aaron said with a proud grin.

"Throughout the first semester I kept track of those who could sing and those who could do other things better. Then I made sure that those who could sing were scheduled into choir classes for second semester. Now we come to those who were lousy singers." He hesitated. "By second semester many of those wanted to be in the choir, too. I told them there was a place for each of them, and they would be important to our concert performances."

"I'm afraid to ask, but do tell me what the non-singers did that was so important to your performances," I asked with a grin.

"I taught one group to be the Umpaws."

"Did you say you taught them to be the 'Umpaws'?" I asked, laughing.

"Sure, you know…umpaw umpaw umpaw paw," he said, as he wriggled his shoulders and snapped his fingers.

"Another group were assigned to be the Do Waws."

"Now I know you're pulling my leg," I said with a louder giggle.

"No, seriously. You know…dowaw, dowaw, diddy diddy dowaw."

"Look, Aaron," I said, chuckling. "You don't really expect me to believe all this?"

"I'm serious," he said, with a bit of a smile. "It actually works, and there's more. We have hand clappers/foot stompers, bell ringers, kazoo players, and other parts as I can come up with them."

"You certainly have my attention," I said. "What do you want from me now, Aaron? And what will you expect in the future?"

"For now, I would appreciate it if you would just visit my classes—and the afterschool choir, when it's up and running. So, you will have a better idea of what I'm hoping to accomplish," he said.

"Well, I plan to do that. You have my attention, and I can promise more support as I observe your program in progress. Were you hoping for more?" I asked. smiling in reassurance.

He took a second before continuing. "That's just for starters. There's a lot more to come," Aaron said. "I have most of the music we will need, but a little later we will need a piano accompanist to prepare for competitions I hope to enter. Entering competitions mean entry fees, and providing transportation, and supervision away from the campus. Like I said, I know I'm asking for a lot. That's why I wanted to talk with you early in the school year, so you would be prepared."

"That is a great deal to think about," I said with a sigh. "You have a lot of lofty ideas. But don't be discouraged; nothing is impossible. I like your enthusiasm. And I like what you're doing for the kids, and I've noticed they really like you. That says a lot for what you have done in just a year's time. I'll begin checking out your classes soon, and we'll need to meet regularly to be ready for those spring programs."

"Does that mean you will support me?" he asked, looking hopeful.

"I am overwhelmed, but I'm intrigued by your goals," I said. "Let's take this a day at a time. Or maybe we will take it a few days at a time. The important thing is that we communicate regularly." I met his relieved gaze. "Don't run off half-cocked getting into something that I'm not aware of, and then expect me to support you in something I normally would not."

"You have my word. Thanks for hearing me through, and for the encouragement. Now, I had better get to my first-period class so I won't be the tardy teacher." He rose from his chair and hurried out to the hallway.

As things calmed down, I was able to visit his classes a little more often. I even spent more time during those visits learning about his program and supporting him with the students. It was obvious that they enjoyed their choir groups. Almost immediately his afterschool, mixed choir grew so large that I arranged for him to meet with them in the auditorium. Besides providing more places for choir members to sit and using the stage, they could get a sense of how it felt to be performers.

***

Early in October, Aaron appeared in my office again asking for help with a catchy issue. "Hey, Lucy, do you think we could get away with having a Christmas program…if we called it something like 'Home for the Holidays'?"

"I didn't even hear you ask, Aaron," I said quickly "You know the district policy is no recognition of any spiritual group."

"Yes, I know, but this Jewish boy loves Christian music," he countered. "Most of the kids in this brown-skinned community are of the Catholic faith. I figure if we do this right, we can get away with it. The community will love it."

"How do you expect to accomplish that? You're sending me mixed messages," I said with a frown.

"If we use a Winter Wonderland theme and call it 'Home for the Holidays' or something like that, we can make it work," he said with determination.

"All I can say right now, Aaron, is show me your plan on paper, including the exact songs that will be sung. When I have that in my hands—if I approve of it, I'll show it to Duane. You realize he has to approve it, too. He and I are the ones with our necks on the line if something goes wrong," I reminded him, equally serious.

Two days later Aaron was back in my office, 'Home for the Holidays' plan in hand. "I know you're going to like this. It's special! Our kids will make it beautiful!"

"You'll have to leave the plan with me because I don't have time to go over it now. Just don't count your chickens before they hatch."

He left my office with both hands raised high with fingers crossed. As he went through the door, he called back, "You're going to love it."

What I didn't know was that Aaron's classes had been practicing Christmas songs for weeks. I looked over his plan carefully, then leaned back and closed my eyes. I tried to think of an approach which might encourage him, but not get our school into hot water. The plan was a good one. In fact, it was very lofty. I made copies of it and took one with me.

When I went into Duane's office, I handed him Aaron's plan. "You're probably not going to like this. You may even feel that we have to turn Aaron down flat. But I believe it is a well thought out program. Under Aaron's supervision, I think it could be a great concert for the students and for the community."

"Sit down, Lucy. I know he is one of our most talented teachers." He sat at his desk and scanned the plan.

After a few minutes, he said, "Before we begin talking about Aaron's program, let me tell you a little about the community you're working in now. As you know, we are considered to be a low-income, disadvantaged community. Here at Eastland School, our population is almost 65% Mexican-American and about 25% Asian. That other 10% is mostly what we call minority groups. Because of that, we still get away with special events which larger districts—like Los Angeles proper—would not be able to. Even our high schools continue to introduce small amounts of what we would call 'spirituality' into seasonal programs."

He looked thoughtful. "Aaron has taken on a terrific challenge here. With the support he has already developed in our school community, I believe he can carry this off. You will have to work with him closely, to make sure he makes no grave errors that are offensive to any group. But I would say let's go for it. Eastland needs a little boost in status. This might help us get moving in that direction."

I smiled, relieved. "I'm surprised, but delighted. I know Aaron will be, too. We'll keep our fingers crossed and plan to give him all the support he needs, as long as he continues to toe the line."

"Great, Lucy, let's do it."

That afternoon I caught Aaron at the end of one of his classes, and I gave him the news. Again, I cautioned him about the importance of keeping dialogue open between the two of us. He promised me that he would do that.

***

It seemed that every time I saw Aaron he had something new and exciting to report. He had enlisted a group of mothers, who promised to help with costumes for a few of the numbers. He had approached the manager of a nearby wholesale store about providing Santa hats, fake snow, and tinsel. He would pick those up at the end of the week.

For weeks, holiday music could be heard throughout the campus on a regular basis. Kids who were not in class with Mr. Leibowitz were humming and singing tunes in small groups as they moved around the campus. A few teachers began complaining about students being pulled from their classes by him in order to practice with larger groups. For the most part, even the staff was impressed by the positive excitement which permeated the campus.

December arrived and the first dress rehearsal was scheduled for December 10th. All day Mr. Leibowitz's classes met in the auditorium. Some teachers volunteered to help him supervise the large groups during their preparation periods. Parts of the program rehearsed during the daytime, but the big rehearsal was after school. Parents were told that the students would be late getting home that evening, and they needed to provide transportation for those who didn't live nearby.

Until that day I never fully realized the depth of Mr. Leibowitz's skills. Class leaders and parents who had volunteered, provided supervision of students who were not rehearsing at the moment. The very low level of noise within the waiting groups was amazing. The rehearsal went well. The soloists were in their special costumes, and regular choir members were in school clothes. He managed to direct them through the program from beginning to end in only 2 ½ hours. He made a few corrections on the spot, and a paraprofessional followed him around writing down notes about corrections he intended to make during the next week.

A week later, the full-dress rehearsal occurred. I scarcely could believe how well it went. Other staff members agreed that this program was something special.

***

The day of the performance arrived. The air was static with excitement. Even the custodians were excited as they helped finish up decorations in the auditorium. We had a program in the morning for half of the students, and would have another in the afternoon for the other half of the student body. That evening the choir would perform for the community.

As the students filed into the auditorium for the afternoon performance, I stood beside Duane at one of the front entrances. "The performance this morning was wonderful," I said to him. Do you suppose we'll be lucky enough to get through the next two performances just as well?"

"That would be great," he said. "I can't believe how well our students are behaving. I can't think of anything that might go wrong, and I pray that nothing will."

"I'm with you there," I said. We followed students into the back of the auditorium.

The performers were feeling good. They knew they had done well in the morning. The students in the audience were also on their best behavior.

About an hour into the performance, a student from the Boys Vice Principal's office came into the auditorium looking for Duane. He had a note from Bob Brown, the Boys Vice Principal.

Duane opened the note, read it and then passed it to me. The note read: We just got an anonymous phone call saying there is a bomb in the auditorium, and it is set to go off in a half hour. I am working with other office staff trying to identify who among our problem students might have made that call. I'm going to continue working on that. I'll leave it to you and Lucy to decide whether or not to evacuate the auditorium.

"We certainly don't need this right now," Duane said, looking grim. "If we evacuate and then find it is a hoax, we will have thrown our schedule off for no good reason. It will take at least ten minutes to evacuate the building. If we wait too long, and there should happen to be a bomb, we would have a major catastrophe."

"Let's take ten minutes to search the building, and then decide whether or not to evacuate," I suggested. "You search back here in the foyer and the sound booth. I'll go around to the stage area and search there. There really are very few places in this building where a bomb—even a small one—could be hidden. See you in a little bit."

When I arrived backstage, I asked a teacher assisting with supervision to help me search. The performers had been instructed to leave their personal possessions in their lockers. So, except for a few props which we scrutinized, we found no place where a bomb could be hidden.

Back in the foyer with Duane, he and I continued our debate on evacuation. "Do you think it could be under one of the seats in the audience?" he asked.

"As the students filed in, the seats were up. Surely, they would have seen anything unusual under a seat. I don't want to alarm them by asking them to look," I said.

"I vote we continue with the program," he said, trying to sound confident.

"I guess I agree with you at this point, but the next hour and a half is going to be grinding," I said. I could hardly breathe because of the stress level.

We decided to remain at the back of the auditorium. He sent word with a student to Bob Brown, telling him where we were, and asking him to let us know as soon as he had any new information.

After another hour into the program, we were just beginning to relax a little. Then Bob came to the door and motioned for us to go back into the foyer.

"I think I've found the identity of Mr. Anonymous," he said. "Somehow I had an idea that might solve our problem. Picking out three of the boys who had been most recently in deep trouble, I began checking on their status. Guess who I found on the third day of a three-day suspension? Our friend Richard Chow."

"That certainly sounds like a possibility," Duane said, and I agreed.

"But wait, it gets even better," Bob added. "As I walked between buildings on the way over here, I glanced toward the street. Guess who was standing almost behind the garage of the house across the street? Richard Chow. I thought about going after him, but then I realized that would be a waste of my energy. It would give him something to brag about. I just waved to him and smiled big. He moved back behind the garage as I came through the door."

"I would say that solves our problem," Duane said, his expression relieved.

Bob and I agreed. Then Duane and I went back into the auditorium to watch the last few minutes of the program. Bob returned to the office where he was standing on duty.

About 20 minutes later the program ended and everyone filed out of the auditorium unscathed. Duane and I returned to the stage area to congratulate Aaron on another good performance.

"Can you believe two performances down without a hitch?" Aaron asked, pleased.

Duane and I shared a grin.

"The program was perfect, you're right. However, we can't quite say it was without a hitch," I said. "Come to the office after school and we'll tell you about the hitch."

"It's almost laughable now," Duane said and mopped his brow. "But nobody was laughing during the last hour and a half. We'll see you later, Aaron. I know you're getting ready for this evening's performance. So, if you would prefer, we can delay our little talk until tomorrow. That's up to you."

Aaron looked concerned, but nodded. "You're right, Boss, I have several things to do before the evening performance. I'll get back with you tomorrow. Thanks."

That evening was the big performance for the community. Even the Superintendent of Schools came with his family, which I'd been told rarely happened. I didn't know whether to consider it good or bad. Had he come to honor us? Or had he come to criticize us for producing a program which went against the district's rules?

By the end of the evening program, I was worn to a frazzle—as were the other administrators and those who had volunteered. We were all excited about how well the whole thing had gone. The superintendent stopped by Mr. Leibowitz to tell him he had never seen the Umpaws and the Doodle Does done so well. Even a reporter and a photographer from the local newspaper appeared during the evening show. As a result, we made the front page of the morning paper the next day.

Eastland had made it big! When everyone was out of the building, Aaron and I left together. As we reached the parking lot, he said, "We're on our way. Wait till you see what I'm planning for spring."

"I'm too tired to think of that now. Go home and rest," I said with a smile.

"Are you sure you don't want to stop by for a drink? I know a good place not too far away," he said, as he held my car door open for me.

"No, Aaron. I know you're excited. I'm sure you have better people to drink with." I yawned. "I'm exhausted. I'm going home and putting my feet up. I'll see you tomorrow."

I gave him a pointed look. "You do remember we have one more day to go before Christmas vacation. Again, let me say I'm very proud of you and the kids. This was an exceptionally great program, and I know many others left with that same opinion. Thanks for a job well done."

On Tuesday of the week following the winter vacation, Aaron was waiting at my office door when I arrived in the morning. "I think we're ready to take our show to a competition. East Los Angeles College is scheduled to host a choral competition for middle schools from the eastern half of the county. It's on March 12, with an Irish St. Patty's day theme. That's right up our alley. What do you think?"

I smiled at him. "Good morning to you, too, Aaron. Now, what exactly are you asking me for?"

He waved a piece of paper at me. "I have here in my hand an application form, and it must be signed by an administrator. When we send it in, we have to provide them with a check for the $50 entry fee. How's that for starters?"

"I've got to have coffee, Aaron," I said. "Leave the application and I'll take a look at it later today. That's all I can promise at this point. Can you live with that?"

"I'll consider that a maybe." He put it on my desk, meeting my gaze. "I'll keep my fingers crossed till I hear from you."

The whole process was easier than I thought it would be. I suspect that had a lot to do with the success of our holiday program.

***

On the day of the competition everything went smoothly. Since the college was within a couple of miles, supervision and transportation were not the big problems they would be for competitions held at places farther away. We competed against 11 other schools and at the end of the day our mixed choir placed third, which entitled us to an award of $200. Our choir members were excited beyond words, but no one was happier than their choir director Mr. Leibowitz.

They also came home with a small trophy, which was immediately placed in the trophy case in the administration building. This was a big deal because until then only athletic trophies had been placed there.

The following morning Mr. Leibowitz arrived early and stayed in the main office almost until school started, allowing staff and students to congratulate him on a job well done. He was one proud Papa. Following me into my office when I arrived, he said excitedly, "Now comes the big one."

I sighed. "Aaron, you know I'm very happy for you, and proud of all that you have helped our young people accomplish. They really have begun to make their mark in Los Angeles County. I'm assuming that by the 'big one' you mean the countywide competition. As I recall, that takes place in May."

"You got it, Boss," he answered.

"How long do we have to get ready for that contest?" I asked, trying not to feel concerned.

"It's scheduled for May 21st and 22nd. That's a month before school lets out for summer recess."

"If I'm right," I said, "that gives us exactly two months to prepare."

He nodded.

"Well, Aaron, the ball is in your court. I cannot begin working on it until I see your written plan. And until we've had a chance to go over it together."

"I'm sending the ball to your court right now. Here's my written plan," he said with a grin, as he placed an envelope on my desk. "I'm ready to schedule an appointment with you to discuss where we go from here. Can we do that now?"

Patience, I need patience. "I swear, no one around here keeps my nose to the grindstone more than you do. If I didn't like what you do so much, I wouldn't allow that to happen. Most of all, I love what you're doing for our special children."

With that in mind, I softened. "Since I want you to keep it up, I guess I'd better get off the dime and move on to the next step. I know your schedule is full, and, at this point, mine is, too. I have supervision during first lunch. I think you have a class at that time. Could we eat lunch together in the cafeteria during second lunch? I'll bring your plan and we'll turn it into an action plan."

IN SEARCH OF THE MAGICAL BOX
Tom Elman

This is an excerpt from a fictional novel that I wrote. The novel is about a boy who finds a magical box. In order to use the magic of the box, he must hide the box, and his dad and sister must find it. So he hides the box for his father to find. And then his father hides it for his sister to find.

Just so you know who is who, I'm going to fill you in on the characters.

Kevin Martin (aka Kev): The boy is thirteen years old, all boy, and left-handed.

Virginia Martin (aka Ginya): The sister has a mind like an encyclopedia.

Bob Martin: The dad is a high school History teacher/basketball coach, and right-handed. He and Kevin are avid metal detector enthusiasts.

Jonus Bird (deceased): The past—passed if you like—owner of the box.

Stix: The dog is a good-sized German Shepherd who can talk to the readers of the novel.

Muse: The cat is a very sarcastic calico, who can also talk to the readers.

Window, Indiana: Locale in 1984

(*) An indication for the occasional notations by the author.

The following excerpt from Chapter Twelve begins at breakfast the day before Bob is to search for the box.

Mischievousness

The next morning at breakfast Kevin repeated how it would be possible for his dad and sister to get the power to summon the magic. It was really very simple. All he had to do was what Virginia had said the night before: hide the box and have his dad find it.

He had spent most of the night trying to figure out where to hide the box. It needed to involve some real trickery, and, of course, some metal detecting. There would be nice clues and not so nice clues. His mind had raced from one location to the next. He'd been reminded of finding instructions that someone had written in one of his used school books. He'd been instructed to go to a certain page, and then told to go to another page and another page and so on. The search had ended when he came to the page that said something like "Hey, stupid, get busy and stop wasting time."

He was meant to do this, to trick the trickster. This was his chance to get even for all the tricks and shenanigans that his dad had played on him for years. Karma was so sweet. It was "comeuppance" time. Then, if his dad ever found the box, his dad would have to hide it for Virginia. Then all three would be able to summon the magic.

"Well, Dad, I am going to hide the box for you to find. If you ever do find it, you will need to hide it for Ginya to find." Kevin flashed his widest, Cheshire Cat smirk.

"I smell a rat. There is some real mischief in that boy's smile. I like it. He's going to make Jonus proud." Stix danced in crazy circles.

"I see the pooch already knows there is some skullduggery in what Kev's hidden agenda may entail. I always thought that she knew a lot more about what we were saying and doing than we thought she did." Virginia smiled at Stix. "You sly ole dog you."

"Wow! That's twice I've been told that now. Maybe they will pay a little more attention to me from now on. Especially around chow time." Stix winked at Virginia.

"What about me, roomie? You think I'm just a dumb calico?" Muse jumped up on Virginia's lap, gave her a wink, and rubbed her face under Virginia's chin.

"Oh my gosh! This is going to be a whole new ball game from here on." Virginia grabbed Muse, stood up, and spun around in circles with the cat tucked under her chin.

After three spins, Muse jumped down. "Enough is enough. I'm not real fond of spinning in circles." She ran out of the kitchen and headed up the stairs. At the top of the stairs, she stopped to lament, "I just hope the new ball game includes an improvement in the cat cuisine around here."

"When will I be able crack this case of the hidden box mystery, my boy?" Kev's dad asked, drawing his attention again.

"I have some of the things pretty well thought through. Although there are a few more twists that I have to work out. Probably tomorrow morning." He looked hopefully at his dad. "Wanna shoot some baskets this morning?"

"HORSE. To see who cleans the scum off the pond?" his dad asked, with a teasing glimmer in his eyes.

It was like a lightbulb flashed over Kevin's head. "You're on! Let's play match it, and it's a letter?"

"Okay, Kev. 'Match it' is alright with me." He hesitated, then added, "How about let's also make it so that you need to prove it if the second shooter misses the shot."

"Alright, Dad! That's what I'm saying. You're coming to play in my house." Kevin grinned with confidence.

"You better bring your best game, young man."

Kevin all but bounced in excitement as he went to the backyard arena with his dad. He should probably feel guilty about leaving Virginia behind to clean up the breakfast things. But he didn't. And he was pretty sure after kitchen duty, she would go upstairs to finish reading the end of one of her Little House on the Prairie books…again.

Let the Games Begin

Kevin spent the rest of the day—after cleaning the pond—preparing and hiding the clues for his dad's search for the box. When he came into the house after dark, Stix was at his heels. After devouring whatever he found eatable in the refrigerator, he headed up to his room to make some last-minute preparations. He curled up in his big pillow bed, a smile on his face as he drifted off to wherever tonight's dreams would carry him.

After breakfast the next morning, the three of them sat around the kitchen table.

"Okay, young man. Where do I start this amateur scavenger hunt?" his dad finally asked.

"Not so fast, Dad. There are rules to be followed." Kevin met his gaze in challenge.

"Good! Lay um on me, young'n." He smirked and winked at Virginia. "By the way, did you get all the yucky stuff out of the pond?"

Kevin rolled his eyes, and then nodded yes to the pond jab. He started instructing with, "Rule one. And this is the most important rule. No Stix!"

"Oh! I'm heartbroken. You think I would ever betray you, Kev? Well, on the other hand, I do have a weak spot when it comes to keeping a secret." Stix licked her lips. "Especially if any food is involved in the relinquishing of information. I think it's a family flaw around here. But good call with rule one, my boy."

Kevin grinned at Stix for a second, wondering what went through her mind. Putting the thought aside, he said, "Rule two. No Ginya."

"Oh my! I feel I'm being besieged by a case of the vaapoors. Does my darling little bruddah think I would abet the leading trickster of Window? Think otherwise." Virginia had the back of her hand to her forehead and had feigned a faint. Then she gave an approving smile. "A very good call on rule one."

"Just covering all my bases. Dad, you might need to get some smelling salts for Scarlet." Kevin scoffed and then glanced away from her. "Rule three. All hints are ten dollars a piece, and I might mention that the hints could be of a very questionable reliability. Capiche?"

His dad nodded, with a grin of amusement. "Why am I not surprised about that? Any more rules? Or are we finally going to get this started?"

Kevin chuckled. "That's all I've got for now. But should the 'status quo' change, there may be some more rules added to rectify the situation at hand. Said the boy whose father often remembered something that he forgot to mention to us when we were doing one of his amateur scavenger hunts."

"Touché," his dad said, his eyes glimmering with appreciation and enjoyment.

"Go get your detector and digging tools. Then meet me at the front door."

Kevin headed in that direction, while his dad went out to the garage to get his things. A few minutes later they are all standing on the front porch.

"Here's the first clue." Kevin handed his dad a folded piece of paper.

His dad opened it and read…

CLUE #1

In Jonus' yard the signal will be
a quarter and in open ground.

As Kevin and Virginia watched, their dad went off the steps and headed down the street towards Jonus' house.

"Can I follow him and record this hysterical historic event for our grandkids, Kev?" Virginia asked in a mocking tone.

"Knock yourself out, Ginya." He looked down at Stix, giving her a warning shake of his head. "Don't even think about going."

Stix laid flat down on porch, gazing up at Kevin. "I am your familiar and you are my master."

Kevin chuckled at the resigned expression on Stix's face.

***

It didn't take much more than fifteen minutes for Bob to get a quarter signal at a depth of less than two inches. He could even see where Kevin had stuck his knife in the grass to pry up just enough dirt and roots to slide in the quarter wrapped in a piece of paper.

He took the paper off the quarter and read…

CLUE #2

Very good, Dad. Now go to the
very clean pond and look for
a red balloon.

Bob picked up the things and headed back home. Slightly amused, he knew that Virginia had taken some nice pictures of his metal detecting skills.

When they got to the back yard and saw that the pool surface was completely covered with two hundred inflated red balloons, they started laughing.

Virginia, of course, took photos from all angles. "Do you have any air left, lil' bruddah?" she taunted him.

Kevin beamed. "I'm pumped to the max." He looked at his dad, smiling even more. "By the way, I'm selling straight pins for a mere five dollars each, if you're in the market, Dad?"

Bob chortled. "Not on your life, Ebenezer. I'll make quick work of these balloons by hand or foot."

He started picking out balloons and bursting them however he could. There was a piece of paper in every one of them. Some pieces had nothing on them. Some pieces said "Nada." Some pieces had arrows pointed to whichever direction he held the paper. But most had paper and pond scum inside. It took him 179 balloons to find the clue which read…

(* Could it be possible that maybe Kevin might have missed that last shot in the game of HORSE with his dad so that he would have undisturbed access to the pond?)

CLUE #3

Did you recheck the hole where
you found the quarter like you
taught me to always do?
Oh! Oh! Oh! Dig deeper.

Bob looked over at Kevin and smiled. Then he observed Virginia, who was bent over in laughter. "Only a father like me would love his son as much as I do right now. Very clever, Kev. Very, very clever."

He focused on his daughter. "Ginya, I think you and I have some reevaluating to do about your brother's capabilities. Well, I guess it's back down the street for me. Come on, Ginya. He probably has some more preparations to attend to."

"Noper! I'm good." Kevin countered cheerfully, drawing Bob's attention again. "And, hey, Dad. Here's one of those rule changes that I said might pop up. You can take Stix with you this time. She helped me dig the hole a little deeper."

"'Tweren't noth'n, folks. It was my pleasure to be of help." Stix trotted along with Bob and Virginia as they headed back to Jonus' house.

When Bob got back to the place where he found the quarter (where Stix was now laying with a paw on each side of where the coin had been buried), he swept his detector over the spot. Sure enough, there was another good quarter signal at five inches deep.

He then realized why Kevin had been so careless with the knife slot that he had used to hide the first quarter. He checked the area within a few inches in each direction from the knife slot. Kevin had very carefully repaired any disturbances of the grass in an eight-inch circle around the first knife slot.

Bob removed the plug of sod and found the second quarter wrapped in paper. Before he opened the clue, he rechecked the hole to possibly eliminate a third trip to Jonus' house. The clue read…

CLUE #4

Come on home and get your
thinking cap on and some paper
and a pencil. Ginya has some
I'm sure she can loan you. I'll
be waiting in the kitchen.

When his dad and Virginia returned, Kevin was sitting at the table with a piece of paper in one hand and a root beer in the other.

Stix walked over and put her head on his leg, seeking his attention. He patted her head.

"He didn't even let me help him just a little bit with the hole like you did, Buddy ole pal-o-mine." She breathed a sigh of frustration, and Kevin palmed her head again, as if he understood.

"Good job covering your plug, young man. So? What's your next trick for me?" his dad asked as Virginia put a pencil and a piece of paper in front of him.

Kevin grinned, feeling confident at the game. "I'm going to ask you some questions, and give you some instructions. It would be good if you took some notes."

Virginia plopped down on her usual chair and gave him a strange stare glare. "Kevin? Do you even know what notes look like?"

"Matters not, Mon Ami. I'm on the other side of the desk right now." He gave her a good-natured glance, then concentrated on his dad once more. "Okay, Dad. The questions. Write down the uniform numbers of these baseball players in the order that I give them to you. Ryne Sandberg, Mickey Mantle, and Ernie Banks. Okay?"

He paused before continuing. "Then put those numbers to the corresponding letters of the alphabet. Write the letters down. I'm not going too fast for you, am I?"

His dad twirled the first two fingers of his hand to indicate "Keep on going. I'm staying with you so far."

Agreeably, Kevin said, "Now then, those letters each have a specific number that is used to identify the broadcast location on Marconi's invention." He took a swig of his root beer and then gazed back down at his instructions. "Lastly, take these numbers and find the corresponding date on our kitchen calendar. That's all folks." He sat up straighter, grinned, proud of himself.

His dad regarded Kevin. "Piece O Cake! Sandberg is #23 and he is going to be one of the best, just like the other two. Mickey was #7. And Ernie will always be the best #14 ever. The #23 is,…give me a sec…W. #7 is G. And #14 is N. That would be WGN. The radio broadcast location is 720. The calendar date would be July 20th." He got up and turned the calendar page to July.

There was a post-it on the 20th. Which read…

CLUE #5

Go to the spot that determined
who had to clean the scum off
the pond. Don't forget your detector.

Bob retrieved his detector and digging tools from the garage, again. He went out the patio door and went directly to the far corner of the yard in amongst the violets and pansies. He saw the very large flagstone that he had stood on to make a left-handed shot that had to go over the corner of the backboard. Which he had swished. When Kevin shot his ball right-handed, it hadn't swished.

He returned to the spot to prove it with another simulated, nothing-but-net swish. Game Over.

It only took a few minutes to move the flagstone and to locate another quarter and the next clue. Which read…

CLUE # 6

*The box is where you usually
do your best tossing and turning.
And also dream up some of
the crazy basketball shots of yours.*

Bob headed straight to his bedroom. He discovered a big lump under the covers in the middle of his bed. He understood that now he could summon the magic.

"Wow! I made seventy-five cents today. And a good time was had by all. How about some lunch? Dot's or the drug store?" he asked, pleased that this part was finished.

"Drug store," Kevin said, sounding ready to go.

"Oh, Kev. You just want to see cutesy-pie Sarah. I vote for Dot's," Ginya teased.

Bob watched in amusement as Kevin frowned in annoyance at his sister. He pulled a coin from his pocket and gave it to Virginia. "Here's a quarter, Ginya. Heads it's Dot's. Tails it's Sarah's."

Virginia held the quarter on edge with the index finger of her left hand and then spun it with a flick of her right index finger.

When it stopped, Kevin gave an arm pump. "Hello Sarah!"

Virginia's Trivia Trial

It was Bob's turn to set up the hunt for Virginia. Neither Virginia nor he wanted this to be easy. But trying to make something tough for her would be very taxing. They were all sitting around the kitchen table again after breakfast when he looked over to her and said, "I also have a few rules that will need to be followed to the letter. Are you ready?"

"Bring it on, Mr. Trickster." She gave him an encouraging look.

"Rule one. You can use Stix if you want."

Stix did circles double time in her excitement. Then she went over and sat down with Team Virginia. "We're going to be awesome together."

Virginia smoothed her head as if in agreement.

"Rule two. You cannot be helped by anyone unless said person is mentioned in the following clues," Bob said, gazing from the eager dog to his daughter.

"Not even my dear sweet brother?"

Bob shook his head, hearing the mischievous note in her voice. "Nada! Rule three. You may not use the car."

Her forehead furrowed. "How far away are these clues? Am I going to need my running shoes?"

"Not real far, but maybe you should wear them," he said, and then reached into his pocket. "Also, here's the seventy-five cents I earned yesterday. And you may need a couple of bucks to loosen some lips."

"Who's all involved in this thing anyway?" she asked, tilting her head curiously.

He grinned, determined to make her use her brain, confident that she could figure it all out. "That's for you to find out. And, finally, rule four is that you can phone home if you need any help."

"Ha! Ha! Like that's going to happen," she said on a snort.

"Okay then, here's the clue to get you going. The clue read…

CLUE #1

There is a car in Window, that is in
plain site, that has a license plate
with the last four numbers 1938. The
owner will give you a clue if you
ask him if the Reds won or lost
their game last night.

"Come on, Stix. Let's go find us a car." Team Virginia left through the front door and headed toward town.

As Bob watched them go, he thought about the car, which he knew belonged to Mr. Bishop. The owner-pharmacist of the drug store had parked his car in the same spot every working day for at least the last twenty-five years. The license plate was always visible from the sidewalk. Bob had talked with him yesterday evening about Virginia's quest. The man was eager to help. After he had listened to suggestions about next year's basketball team, Bob assured him that he would absolutely make good use of those suggestions. He'd agreed that they should be very beneficial to improving the team.

***

As Virginia strode downtown, she realized (per rule #2) she couldn't drop in at city hall to get them to look up the license number for her.

Rule number two just went into effect.

She and Stix cruised down the north side of the street with no luck. They crossed over to the south side and headed east. Stix was ahead of her and then sat down at the corner of the drug store. When Virginia caught up with her, Stix was doing circles again. Virginia noticed that next to her was the car with the license they were looking for.

"Good girl, Stix. This will stay with us. No one will ever be the wiser." She leaned down to give Stix a big hug around her neck.

"We work well together. I hope there's some digging involved in what we're doing!" Stix was bursting with excitement, her tail wagging in anticipation.

Virginia went into the store and stopped at the pharmacy window. "Hi, Mr. Bishop. My dad said you would have a clue for me."

"Clue? Whatever are you talking about, young lady?" He turned as if to be busy with some pills or something.

Blam! A lightning bolt hit her brain as she remembered what the clue had said. "Mr. Bishop? Did the Reds win or lose last night?"

"They won. Now give me a dollar and you can have your clue," he answered with a pleased look of understanding.

Virginia reached into her pocket and then handed him a dollar bill. "Thank you." She gave him a little smile and went back out where Stix sat by the door. She read the clue which said...

CLUE #2

Go to Dot's Diner and ask 'DOT' for
a small ginger ale. Sit at one of the
booths and she will bring it to you.

163

Stix and Virginia walked to the end of the street and then crossed an open field to get to the diner just off the main street. Excited, Stix thought this place had some eligible spots for some real digging to be done by Window's best digger. But no luck today. Virginia used their route simply as a short cut—via a well-worn dirt path—to the diner.

Leaving a saddened Stix outside, Virginia went into the diner. She found Dot at the cash register, and—per the instructions—asked if she could have a small ginger ale.

"Coming right up, young lady." Dot's eyes shone with amusement. Virginia assumed it was because her dad had asked for Dot's help. The older woman had been in on some of his other shenanigans. She was a good sport. But she'd probably talked to her dad about getting Rick Johnson to shoot more from the outside in the next basketball season. Everyone in town seemed to have some kind of advice for her father.

"Have a seat at that booth and I'll have it for ya in a jiffy." Dot glanced through the front door. "That's sure a mighty pretty dog you have waiting out there."

"That she is," Virginia said with a smile and took a seat in the booth. A couple of minutes later, Dot brought over her drink and placed it on a napkin. She put another napkin off to the side of the drink.

Virginia thanked her and took a drink of her soda. She considered the clue from Mr. Bishop. She had noticed before that the word 'DOT' was made with a magic marker. Why?

As she glanced at the other napkin, she saw that it also had 'DOT' written on it with a magic marker. It looked like the same person had written both clues. She picked up the napkin and found another clue stuck on the other side. Which read…

CLUE #3

Play B-4 on the jukebox. Near the end of the song, the singer will tell you where the next clue is. Listen very closely. You may need to listen a few times. Don't forget rule four.

164

Virginia paid for her ginger ale and went to put a quarter in the jukebox, pushing B-4: Rhinestone Cowboy by Glen Campbell. She listened to a song that she had heard many times. But when it ended, she still didn't know where to look for the clue.

She had two more times to play the song on her quarter. This time she hovered right next to the jukebox and tried to close out all other noises in the diner. The song ended as she finally caught the words "over the phone." Excitedly, she spun around and looked at the pay phone. She smiled to herself as she remembered rule four. There was a big 'DOT' over the phone.

"Ha! I don't need no stinking rule four." She hurried to the phone and took the sign with the next clue attached. As she started for the door to leave, she turned to Dot and said, "Thanks, Dot, and you got a freebee on your jukebox."

Outside, she gave Stix a pat for being so patient and well behaved. She opened the clue which read…

CLUE #4

Go to the high school tennis court and find the ball with the next clue.

The high school just happened to be a half mile outside the other side of town. Virginia understood now why her dad had suggested running shoes. She hoped that she would see someone she knew going that direction, but threw that idea out as soon as she remembered rule number two.

Off she and Stix loped across the field, and then headed west, staying on some of the back streets.

⋆⋆⋆

Bob got Dot's phone call telling him that Virginia had figured the clue out on the second try. She told him his daughter was on her way to the high school. Pleased with the news, he thanked her and said that they would be coming in tonight for the prime rib special.

For the next part of his plan, he had managed to find about two hundred tennis balls in all variations of conditions. He and Kevin had them in the trunk of the car.

They quickly drove to the high school, and then began tossing the balls to all corners and everywhere else on one of the courts.

"I'm going to shoot some hoops 'til you see her coming up the road." Kevin turned to go.

"Okay, Kev. I'll keep a watch out." He smiled at his son, then added in amusement, "I'll bet Stix is the first one here."

***

Virginia jogged up the road from the highway, with Stix leading the way. When Kevin whistled, Stix broke into a full out sprint for the tennis courts.

"You turncoat, Stix. I thought we were a team," she complained.

She got to the tennis courts and saw her dad and Kevin sitting on a bench inside of one of the courts. Stix was plastered against Kevin's leg. Virginia smiled across the court and nodded. "Used one of Kev's little tricks didn't you, Dad?"

He grinned. "I never was one to let a good thing go to waste."

She walked out on the court and picked up the nearest ball. Nothing was on it. She turned toward her dad and Kevin. "Nothing?"

They both shrugged their shoulders and just looked at her.

She flipped the ball over her shoulder and picked up another one. Nothing. She tossed it away, and before it even hit the ground, she realized her grand mistake.

Facing them again, she put up her hand to silence anything they might be about to say. She then put her finger to her head like a gun and snapped her thumb forward.

They didn't say a word.

As she picked up ball after ball after ball, she placed them where she knew that she wouldn't have to pick them up again and again.

Stix rejoined Team Virginia and helpfully brought her ball after ball. They searched every nook and cranny of the court. When she was satisfied that there were no more balls left to find, she walked slowly toward her dad and Kevin.

Kevin was spinning his basketball on one of his fingers. As the ball turned, she saw the irregular color flash past.

She ran over and flicked the ball off his finger, and then picked it up and took the clue off the ball. Handing the ball back to him, she patted him on top of his head. "Good one. Whose idea yours or Dad's?"

"Dad wanted me to just set the ball down by the bench. I added the spinning." He smirked, clearly proud of himself.

Her dad rolled his eyes at her brother. Ready to move on, Virginia opened the clue which read…

CLUE #5

Time to go home and get ready
for your trivia brain teasers. And
to beware of the master tricksters.

Soon they were all back at the kitchen table with drinks and pieces of a very delicious strawberry rhubarb pie that Grandma Martin had brought over while Virginia was out collecting clues around town. Bob had a legal-sized pad in front of him. Virginia had paper and a pencil in front of her, too. Kevin was reading a Richie Rich comic book.

Bob focused on Virginia. "You've done a great job so far. I'll refund the money that you paid for my Cubs losing to Mr. Bishop's Reds and your ginger ale." He grimaced. "I really thought that the song might stump you, and you would have to phone home."

Virginia said smugly, "Rule four clicked in when I listened the second time."

Kevin glanced up, eyes flashing with mischief. "Dad! I told you that I always thought there was something built into her brain when she was born. How else could she remember all that stuff?"

"Want to see my notes on the rules?" Virginia asked in challenge, pinning her brother with a pointed look.

"No!"

"Enough!" Bob decided to end their little squabble. "Ginya, I have the next part of your quest on this pad. There are ten questions that cover ten different areas of knowledge. You will need to correctly answer eight of the ten questions in order to pass. I know that 80% is not a real good score for you to aim for, but I'm taking into consideration the type of questions and the authors of them."

He glanced at the pad and back up. "Some will be a snap for you. Some will test your knowledge. Some will test your ability to make sure that you interpret the exact wording and meaning of the questions." He hesitated for emphasis. "Take your time and remember who made up the questions. Any questions before you start?"

"What resources do I get to use?" Virginia asked, sounding serious.

"You can use anything at this table, including Kev and Stix, but not me."

"Oy vey! I don't think I'll need either of those two kibitzers." She laughed. "So, in other words, I'm on my own." She held out her hand. "Give me the pad and let's get this over with."

"Roger Wilco!" Bob gave her the pad, ready for her to get started, too.

These are her questions...

(*Dear readers, I encourage you to write down your own answers, to see how well you did on Virginia's test. Good luck.)

1.   Science

The longest day of the year in the US of A is called?

____ A. The vernal equinox.

____ B. Ground Hog Day.

____ C. The winter solstice.

____ D. The summer solstice.

____ E. The last day of school before summer vacation.

2.   US History

List four signers of the Declaration of Independence.

_____

_____

_____

_____

3.   English

Which is the proper possessive pronoun?

____ A. They'res

____ B. There's

___ C. Theirs

___ D. Them's

___ E. Their's

4.   Biology

Match the term with the meaning.

___ Aerobic   A. Born with

___ Catalyst   B. Lil' Bruddah

___ Terrestrial   C. Disease causing

___ Pathogen   D. Requires oxygen (other than Spazz)

___ Spazz   E. Pertains to land

___ Innate   F. Speeds a chemical reaction

5.   Home Economics

Match the Conversions.

___ 1 gallon   A. a pound

___ 1 quart   B. 3 teaspoons

___ 1 cup   C. 8 ounces

___ 1 pint   D. an attention getter

___ 1 tablespoon   E. 4 quarts

___ 1 pinch   F. 2 pints

6.   US State Capitals

Pronunciation – what is the correct way to pronounce the capital of Kentucky?

____ A. Loui ville.

____ B. Louis ville.

____ C. Lou ville.

____ D. Lou a ville.

____ E. Huey-Dewey-Louie ville.

____ F. Add your own pronunciation.

7.   Music

Match terms and meanings.

____ Acappella   A. Repeat a verse

____ Largo   B. Instrumental

____ Sonata   C. To carry on to the next without a pause

____ Reprise   D. Noise

____ Segue   E. Slow

____ Kev's music   F. Without instruments

8.   Geology

From base to summit, what is the tallest mountain in the world?

____ K2

____ Danali (Mt. Wilson)

____ Mauna Kea

____ Mt. Everest

____ Mt. Kilimanjaro

____ Kev's dirty laundry basket

9.   Land Measures

Match the Conversions.

____ Acre   A. 10 feet

____ Yard   B. 3 miles

____ Meter   C. 43,560 ft. squared

____ Mile   D. 3 feet

____ Basketball rim height   E. 1.09 yards

____ League   F. 1,609 meters (approx.)

10.   Math/Algebra (I saved the best for the last and, by the way, this is Kev's question.) Solve this equation by turning each part into a common everyday word or letter. The answer is something you (Virginia) did today. Good luck!

$$\sqrt{-1} \quad 2 \text{ cubed} \quad \Sigma \quad \pi$$

It took Virginia about 15 minutes to finish. After rechecking and then changing one of the answers, she handed the pad over to Bob with a flourish. "Ta Daaa!"

He checked through her answers and then went back to the first question. "Your answer to question one…" He showed the pad of questions to Kevin. "Is a very clever drawing of yourself with a circle around the 21st of June on the calendar. 'Summer Solstice.'"

"No problem with Adams, Franklin, Hancock, Jefferson. By the way, which Adams?"

"Both. John and Samuel," she said with a self-satisfied grin.

He nodded and studied the pad again. "Theirs was your answer, which is correct. But why not their's?" he asked, pretty sure he couldn't trip her up.

"Thanks to our English teacher Mr. Chin. Their's is non-existent, and neither is your's," she answered with confidence.

"Did you have any problems with the Biology terms?" (The answers were D, F, E, C, B, A.) He knew she wouldn't have, but he had to ask.

She laughed. "Pretty easy. Terre…earth. Aero…air. Blah, blah, blah."

"Very good." His daughter was so smart. "And I didn't think there would be any problem with the Home Economics questions." (Her answers were E, F, C, A, B, D.)

"Yeah. Pretty basic. But Mrs. Woodruff would have also accepted 'accent' for a pinch."

He met her amused gaze, amused himself. "I thought I would fool you on the Kentucky capital."

She shrugged. "You did for a while. Then I remembered our visit to one of your college buddies last summer at that beautiful little college in central Kentucky…Berea College." She looked thoughtful. "I also remember that it was the first inter-racial, co-educational college in the U.S. of A. We drove through Louisville, Frankfort, and Lexington on the way. I also remembered the big sign saying, 'Welcome to Frankfort The Capital Of The Commonwealth Of Kentucky.' You had me guessing on that question for a little while."

It made him proud that he had managed to make her think hard at least on one question. She wasn't easily fooled. "I put that question in for a couple of simple reasons. I wanted to see if you had paid attention to the places we passed through while I was driving. And, secondly, I wondered if you had any thoughts about going to college at Berea."

Virginia took a second, then said, "I'm pretty sure that I will either go to Huntington College or Ball State. But I haven't crossed Berea off my list of possibilities."

Bob looked over at Kevin. "Do you have any memories of that trip, Kev?"

"Yeah. I remember all the tobacco plants growing along the roads. I didn't see any blue grass." He grinned. "And I kept watching to see Dan Issel and Louie Dampier playing one-on-one on a playground. But no such luck."

"And again, Dad, the root words made the answers to the music questions simple," Virginia said, grabbing his attention again. (Her music questions answers were F, E, B, A, C, D.)

"I see there was some indecision on the mountain question." Bob glanced at the pad, and then back at his daughter. "You changed your answer from Mt. Everest to Mauna Kea. Which is the proper answer. What made you change your mind?"

"Well, I know Mt. Everest is the highest mountain. But as I reread the question again and again, I knew the trickster was at work." She gave him a meaningful look. "Then I remembered something from the Geography/ Geology mini course that you taught when we were doing those between semesters micro-electives. You remember those?"

At his nod, she continued, "They were like the 9-week phase-elective classes that we tried when I was a sophomore. Except these only lasted five days. Anyway, you talked about the 137 islands that made up the Hawaiian Archipelago. You said they were all formed from one volcanic hotspot that created one massive mountain. So, I guessed that Mauna Kea was the tallest from sea floor to peak." She thrust out her chin, obviously proud of herself.

Bob was proud of her, too. "Good guess. I assume the land measures were of little problem to you." (Her answers were C, D, E, F, A, B.) He raised an eyebrow. "But I see your answer to the final question is not completed."

She looked aggravated. "I know. I know the last three parts…eight(ate), sum(some), Pi(pie). But I have no idea what the square root of minus one is. Three ate some pie. Two ate some pie. One ate some pie."

"Bingo! Close enough. You ate some pie." Kevin gave a fisted arm pump, bouncing with excitement in his seat.

"I ate some pie is the answer?" Virginia questioned, sounding confused.

"Yepper! Even though I never plan to use Algebra again." He glanced at Bob. "Dad, it's not that I don't like math. I just don't like it when they mix in the alphabet with the numbers. But I did remember that the answer to the square root of minus one is represented as a lower-class cursive 'i'. Voila! I ate some pie."

Bob smiled with approval at his son. "I'm proud of you for that, Kev." Gazing at his daughter, he said, "And, Ginya, I'm giving you a 95% on the test. Which means you receive the next clue."

He handed her the clue. Which read…

CLUE #6

*Just as I found the box in my
bedroom…you will be able to
locate the box in a much Wilder
spot in your room.*

Virginia hurried out of the kitchen and headed up the stairs with her entourage close behind. There wasn't a big hump in her bed, as there had been in her dad's room. But there were some things out of place.

Well…three things were out of place. Muse wasn't on the bed, and Muse's blanket wasn't on the bed, either. Over in the corner of the room, she spotted a pile of something covered by the blanket. Muse was curled up on top.

Seeing Virginia, Muse stood, stretched, and then arched her body into the shape of a horseshoe. "It's about time you got here, sweet girly. And who invited that slobbery dog into our room? Yuk!"

Virginia watched Muse hop up onto the bookcase and then onto the dresser. Then she jumped down to the bed without ever disturbing a single figurine or brush or barrette along the way. "Impressive," she said to the cat.

Remembering why she had come here, she looked around the room again. The pile. She walked over and lifted the blanket and found every one of her Little House on the Prairie books sitting on top of the box. "That's Wilder," she said, ecstatic at her discovery.

She understood that now she also had the power to use the magic.